Tanner's Lottery

By Glen Sample

Table of Contents

Produced in the United States of America

First release 2016

Sample Graphics
12381 Pine Street
Garden Grove, CA 92840

Chapter 1

The Night Shift

Tanner Riley sat back in his chair and with a few clicks of the mouse shut down his computer. It had been a long day. Looking at the clock, he couldn't believe it was already 2:30 in the morning.

Down the hallway, Sandy, his wife of five years slept in their warm bed, expecting him to join her hours ago. He undressed and brushed his teeth while examining the dog-tired face staring back at him in the bathroom mirror.

"I look like hell," he thought, splashing warm water on his face. His ability to slip into bed without Sandy waking had been finely tuned and, this time, proved to be no exception. In the morning she would ask, "What time did you get to bed last night babe?" and he would lie, "Around midnight."

Lying in bed, he forced himself to close his eyes, starting the slow process of winding down from his project that had been consuming every evening. Though he was exhausted, it was a good kind of tired. As he turned and patted his warm Sandy, fast asleep beside him, he reasoned his work to be well worth the temporary neglect she had been experiencing.

Fading towards sleep, Tanner's thoughts drifted back to college, where he and Sandy dated. She had always been the catalyst in his life and career; ever-loyal and always supportive.

Sandy was the altruistic one, who graduated from nursing school at the top of her class. Tanner, the math nerd, sat at the other end of the spectrum. As an actuarial analyst for a large insurance company, he loved working with numbers, and Sandy loved saving the world. Her career as a research nurse at Children's Hospital of Orange County had become the main focus of her life, but in spite of these differences, or perhaps because of them, their relationship remained strong. Tanner's thoughts of Sandy brought a smile to his face that sleep did not erase.

***

Tuesday morning came much too early for Tanner. By the time he became alert, it was already 6:45 and Sandy was preparing to leave for her nursing shift.

"You pulled another all-nighter, huh?" Sandy asked as she gave him a hurried kiss on his cheek.

"Yeah, but you'll be happy to know that I finally finished the list in time for the lottery draw tonight."

"So, does this mean you'll be getting more than four hours of sleep from now on?" asked Sandy.

"We'll see. I've got a really good feeling about tonight," Tanner said confidently. He decided to dismiss Sandy's barb about his sleep patterns.

Sandy knew this was important to him. Tanner's experimenting with lottery numbers was going into its third year. She officially labeled him 'truly obsessive' after the first three months of trial and error. To Sandy, the matter was clear: one simply cannot consistently predict the winning lottery number.

"There are just too many possible combinations!" she would say. "You would have to buy 41 million lottery tickets to come up with the winning number!"

She had often argued that all of his late night number-crunching was a waste of time.

"That's why you're the nurse and I'm the math wiz, my dear," Tanner would reply.

But on this morning, there would be none of that. Sandy was through being the practical one – the naysayer. Tonight would be the night when one of them would savor the "I told you so" victory, and she wondered if it would be Tanner. She had never seen a man more driven, more passionate about numbers, so, perhaps he was right. Maybe his theory about number patterns was valid after all.

Tanner had tried to explain to Sandy, in simple terms, about his theories.

"Think of it this way, Sandy," Tanner would say, "If there are 41 million combinations of lottery number choices, who would stand the best chance of winning – the player who buys one ticket or the player who buys 10,000 tickets?"

"Well, of course you would have a better chance by playing 10,000 tickets," Sandy agreed, "but you would still lose."

"What if you bought 250,000 tickets? Would you feel a little more confident about choosing the winning number?" Tanner asked.

"A person would have to be nuts to spend a quarter of a million dollars on lottery tickets," she would say.

"That's exactly where my formula of number patterns comes into play. I agree that buying 250,000 randomly picked numbers would be a waste of money. Random numbers are useless numbers. But certain numbers can be identified as 'pattern numbers' – in other words, some numbers over a period of weeks and months tend to fall into patterns. Some patterns are positive, others are negative. My formula grades each of the numbers that are used in the California SuperLotto Plus game – 1 through 47 for main numbers and 1 through 27 for the mega numbers. My program then distills these numbers into 250,000 highly graded number combinations that

3

theoretically hold the best potential to produce the winning lottery number."

Perhaps it was possible. Tonight would be the night. Tanner would put his 'list' up against California's Super-Lotto Plus jackpot, which had grown over the weeks to 76 million dollars. If just one of his 250,000 'distilled' numbers turns out to be the winner, Tanner would be vindicated. The victory would be on paper only, since, as Sandy often reminded him - no one in their right mind would risk purchasing 250,000 lottery tickets based on unproven formulas. Not yet.

Tanner was pouring a cup of coffee when Sandy gathered up her purse and nursing bag and headed for the door. She gave him a peck on the cheek. "I'll see you tonight – I'll bring home some Wong's, OK?" He loved Chinese food.

"Make sure they include the fortune cookies with that order," he chuckled to himself.

He watched her as she walked out the door and down the walkway to her car. She looked great in her fashionable scrubs, but then Sandy looked great in just about anything, he thought. Always appearing tan and shapely, she was a real California girl. Tanner's admiration was halted by the jangling of the phone.

"Hello." Tanner grabbed a notepad and scribbled the caller's instructions.

"Okay, good. 9:30, right?"

His Wednesday morning meeting delay made him happy. An hour difference would make his drive from Huntington Beach to his office in Irvine a little smoother, plus giving him time to have another cup of coffee.

He turned on his laptop and scrolled through a few pages of numbers. Each page was jammed with neat rows of lottery number combinations. If the California Lottery were a religion, this 'list' would be Tanner's bible. He was familiar with every page. Nothing was random; each lottery number earned its place in the list - all 250,000 of them. Somewhere, nestled in this list of computer-generated numbers, was the number that would be drawn tonight at 8 o'clock – or so he hoped. Perhaps the years invested in research and programming would finally be rewarded.

Tanner's three-year career at Pacific States Indemnity as an actuarial analyst "was a great gig," as Tanner would say. His job surrounded him with the elements that he enjoyed the most – math, analytical analysis, computer programming and challenging problem solving. In effect, Tanner was paid to use his love of numbers to make reasonable predictions about unknown future events. He had the perfect job and he knew it. Together, he and Sandy made a comfortable living, allowing them to purchase a modest condominium in Huntington Beach, three blocks from the blue Pacific.

Tanner turned off the laptop and carried it upstairs to his office. Grabbing the edge of a gilded baroque picture frame, he swung it open, revealing a small wall safe. He opened it and deposited the computer inside, then closed and secured the safe. It was time to go to work.

Chapter 2

Laying Low

Mario Gutierrez stood inches taller than most of the other men gathered around the lunch truck. It was early morning and most of the men at the edge of the parking lot of the Home Depot were confident that they would soon be picked up as day laborers. Mario, at 24, was the youngest of the group but usually the one to be chosen first, much to the displeasure of the other men. But the young man was fluent in English, having learned it in his native Mexico, and often would be commandeered to be the interpreter for the older men, who knew little, if any, English. Some of the men wondered why this gifted young man continued breaking his back as a day laborer. Normally, a young illegal such as Mario would be snapped up by an American contractor. But the young laborer, following his instincts, laid low. He wanted to blend in, not stand out. So, day after day he showed up early in the morning, and with the rest of the men, flagged down every vehicle that even resembled a work truck, urging them to hire him. His life depended on keeping a low profile, for he was a wanted man in Mexico; wanted not by the police, but by the brutal Carlos "Fat Man" Flores.

***

Carlos Flores grew up in Tijuana, Mexico in one of the poorest sections of the border city, where entire houses near the river were built with plywood, cardboard and rusty sheets of corrugated sheet metal. His career as a low-level street thug started at age twelve by stealing chickens in his neighborhood and selling them to a local 'wholesaler.' By age 17, he showed a flair for stealing cars from the tourists in his area, from Tijuana, south to Rosarito Beach and Ensenada. Tipping the scales at over 300 pounds, Carlos was also in demand as "muscle" at various clubs and bars in Tijuana. His volatile temper and brute strength became his calling card and he was soon put to work as an intimidator, enforcer, and punisher for the Tijuana Cartel, run by the Arellano Felix family.

In the years to follow, Carlos gained a great deal of respect within the cartel. Besides manifesting an imposing presence, Carlos Flores had developed a long list of criminal talent he brought in to work for the organization. Many of his friends were American citizens, sons of lower middle-class Mexicans, living across the border in Southern California. These young men, who were often street gangsters themselves, frequented the clubs of Tijuana during Carlos' career as 'bouncer'. Carlos would treat his American friends as VIPs and provide them with booze, drugs and women. Some of these men recruited by Carlos helped him set up routes between Tijuana and California, where tons of cocaine, marijuana and meth were smuggled north and millions in cash smuggled south. These were the best 'burros' money could buy – American burros, who came and traveled through the border with impunity; some of them setting up elaborate businesses in Mexico to enhance their trafficking. Carlos Flores made them rich and they made Carlos' operation stand out as solid in the eyes of the Arellano Felix family.

As years went by, the Tijuana Cartel, having enjoyed decades of unhampered operations, felt the pressure of political change. Large-scale operations were being implemented against all of the Mexican cartels by the joint US and Mexican drug task forces. The number of arrests skyrocketed, as long-standing drug routes were discovered and shut down. Soon the pressure reached the top of the Arellano Felix organization. In 2002, Ramon Arellano Felix died in a gun battle with Mazatlan police. Then, later that same year, Benjamin, the patriarch of the family was arrested in Mexico and charged with cocaine trafficking and money laundering violations. Benjamin had been a priority of DEA and Mexican authorities since 1992. It was Benjamin who first saw the criminal potential of young Carlos Flores and trained him as a Lieutenant in the smuggling operations of the cartel.

Then, in 2006, while fishing off the coast of Baja on his boat "Dock Holliday", Francisco Javier Arellano Felix was interdicted by a US Coast Guard cutter in international waters and arrested.

During this time, Carlos Flores kept his team intact and profitable. To his credit, he remained calm and dependable. Had it not been for a single wrinkle in his organization his record would have been perfect, but among gangsters, there will always be a wrinkle – somewhere. It came in the shape of Mario Gutierrez.

Mario Gutierrez evolved into one of Carlos Flores' most promising young soldiers. Fluent in English, ambitious and very street smart, Flores trained Mario to transfer large amounts of cash to Mexico from Southern California and Arizona. Later, Mario was trained to oversee the incoming hoards of cash that came into Mexico near the San Miguel Gate, a veritable freeway of cash, on an Indian reservation in Arizona. But Mario saw an opportunity for sudden wealth and made the mistake of his life. Stuffing a million dollars in $100 bills into a duffle bag, Mario buried the cash in the desert and fled the area, making his way to California. His ill-conceived plan was to wait a year, until the incident became written off as a loss by the cartel, then return to the area to recover his fortune. He failed to consider, however, that Carlos Flores and the Arellano Felix cartel forget little, and write off nothing.

Chapter 3

The Dry Run

Sandy was already home when Tanner pulled his car into their small garage. He retrieved his briefcase from the trunk and walked towards the front door. Pushing the remote, he heard the garage door creaking shut behind him.

"Wow, something smells pretty good in here," Tanner announced, placing his briefcase on the floor and tossing the keys up on the kitchen bar. Sandy had set out dishes and was busily unpacking small cartons of food from a bright red bag labeled "Wong's Chinese Cuisine."

"Wash up babe and let's eat before this gets cold."

Tanner disappeared for a few moments, returning with his laptop computer, which he laid on the coffee table.

"OK, let's get this show on the road," he said, taking his place at the end of the kitchen bar. He reached for the Orange Chicken while Sandy scooped up the pork fried rice. They always ordered Chinese food whenever the time was just right. Neither of them could explain what made the time 'right' for Wong's. It was an unspoken impulse, prompted by a good day at work or an especially good feeling or who knows? Wong's takeout was the result of a unanimous and usually spontaneous decision. The food, always wonderful and fun to eat, was exceptionally good on this evening. The names of the dishes themselves were fun. – Kung Pau Beef, Moo Goo Gai Pan, Egg Foo Young, who could resist? Sandy and Tanner ate until they could eat no more. Washing it down with cold Chablis, they soon bemoaned the quantity of food consumed in such a short period of time.

"Here's your fortune cookie," Tanner said, playfully tossing it to Sandy.

"I don't think there's room for one more bite," Sandy groaned.

Tanner unwrapped his cookie, snapped it in two and pulled out the tiny message.

"You are destined for great wealth."

"How does the cookie know that?" she laughed.

Sandy lobbed her cookie Tanner's way. Tanner caught it and popped it into his mouth.

"Hopefully, tonight will give us a clue as to our being destined for great wealth," Tanner said as he held up the scrap of paper in the air.

"Maybe the cookie's right."

The time for the Super-Lotto drawing was 8 p.m. Tanner was excited as he and Sandy cleaned up the kitchen and boxed up the leftovers. He reached for the laptop he would use to check the California Lottery website.

"We've got about 20 minutes until the draw, I'm going to take a shower and get into my jammies, OK?" Sandy announced.

"Sure babe, hurry up, though."

Tanner didn't want Sandy to miss a minute of the Lottery draw. He clicked on the database containing his number combinations and for the next ten minutes reviewed his data. Everything was as ready as it could be. But was there anything he left out? Was there anything he could have done to enhance his chances for a win tonight? What if there was no winning number tonight? What would he do next? All these questions would have to wait until this evening's lottery draw was concluded.

Tanner then turned to the California Lottery website and clicked on the Super-lotto page. Just then, Sandy appeared, wearing her pajamas and drying her hair with a towel.

"Did I miss anything?" she asked.

"No, we have a few more minutes," Tanner replied.

"Are you nervous?" Sandy asked, moving behind her husband and massaging his tense shoulders.

"I guess you could say I'm hopeful, but yes... definitely nervous."

The Super-lotto draw is videotaped in Sacramento, California at 7:57 p.m. and soon after is made available on the internet. Tanner continued refreshing the 'current results' page until finally, at 8:16 p.m., the winning number appeared. Squinting at the screen, he read: 16, 47, 22, 23, 34 and the Mega number 8. At the bottom of the page was the announcement that there were no jackpot winners in tonight's contest.

Tanner looked up at Sandy, who was still massaging his shoulders.

"All right babe lets plug in the numbers and see what we've got."

Tanner typed in the winning numbers and pressed 'enter'. There was a two-second pause as his database was scanned - then a number appeared in a highlighted box. It was on page 184 of his voluminous list – the number 16-22-23-34-47-8.

"That's it!"

Tanner's voice exploded. He checked the numbers again, repeating them slowly.

"16-22-23-34-47-8 – right?"

"16-22-23-34-47-8 – that's right," shouted Sandy.

"That's my number!" proclaimed Tanner! He had indeed picked the winning Super Lotto number. "We did it, Sandy!"

Sandy sat down beside her husband and placed the laptop on her lap, examining the highlighted number and double checking the results.

"I can't believe it Tanner – you really did do it!" Sandy shouted in astonishment. She wrapped her arms around her stunned husband and kissed him. "I'm so proud of you – you did it!"

Tanner sat mesmerized, staring at the computer screen in disbelief. The enormity of his task, however, did not escape him. From a total of 41,416,353 possible number combinations for tonight's lottery draw, Tanner had mathematically distilled that number to 250,000 – and from that group, the winning number had emerged. Although there would be no tangible cash prize of $76 million, a prize of another sort was awarded on this Wednesday evening. Tanner was rewarded with vindication, and a strong confidence that his patterned number theories were valid.

This formula that had proven successful on this evening had never before been attempted. Coupled with his computer programming skills, Tanner Riley had created the perfect storm.

Tanner insisted on opening a bottle of champagne, a detail that he had planned days in advance by hiding the bottle toward the back of the refrigerator.

"You think of everything, don't you?" Sandy laughed as they sipped champagne and celebrated their victory. It was time to savor the moment.

"What would we do with 76 million dollars?" Sandy asked.

"Anything that you want Sandy – anything." Tanner's voice was assuring and serious. He looked straight into her eyes as he spoke. "What would you like to do?"

"I think I would like to help people – those who really need some serious assistance - who are not as lucky as I am."

Her response reflected what Tanner loved about Sandy. Her desire to help people was what made her choice of nursing a natural one. Her answer to Tanner's question came as no surprise. He knew that her response would be an unselfish one.

Their animated conversation that evening was filled with ideas and possibilities. It made Tanner happy to realize that Sandy, who was formerly skeptical about her husband's formulas and theories, had suddenly become a believer.

Chapter 4

The Pitch

Thursday morning found Tanner awakening to the question of the dream or the reality of last night. It took a minute to emerge from his slumber and recall the details of the previous evening. Tanner threw back the covers and shuffled to the kitchen where his laptop was laying on the kitchen bar. He returned to his program and reviewed page 184, where the winning number - 16-22-23-34-47 was located. Checking closely the columns of numbers above and below the winning number, he noticed similar numbers – the exact same 5 numbers - 16-22-23-34-47, but a different Mega number. Tanner laughed out loud. He had actually won twice. He had also won the secondary prize, worth $38,000.

It was now time for the second phase of Tanner's plan. To do it right, he decided to take the rest of the week off – a rare thing for him to do. He had plenty of personal days owed to him and this would be the best time use them. His first phone call, however, was not to his office. It was much too early for that. He dialed the number of someone he knew would be awake at 6:30 in the morning, Sandy's brother Jonathan Taylor.

"Hello."

"Hey, Jonathan, it's Tanner."

"I know. What's up; is everything OK?"

"Oh sure, everything is fine, how about you?" Tanner asked.

"Doing good buddy, how's my sis?"

"She's doing good - as busy as ever. In fact, I was calling to see if we could get together for dinner sometime this week. It's been a while since we've seen you guys and, well, I've got an idea that I want to run by you."

Jonathan was now curious. It was out of character for Tanner to be the one to set up any social engagement; Sandy had always been the one to initiate family gatherings. And as for any "ideas" that Tanner wanted to bounce off Jonathan, that too was backward. Tanner was one of the brightest people Jonathan had ever known; how could he be of any assistance to Tanner? On countless occasions over the years, it was Jonathan who consulted with Tanner. But it was Jonathan that had the Midas touch. At 22, he had started investing in real estate and at 24 reached the status of multi-millionaire. By parlaying his wealth into investments such as Apple and Google. Jonathan netted a few more million dollars. Now, at 35, he was at his peak.

"I'm leaving tomorrow night for London and I'll be gone for a week; can we get together when I get back?"

Tanner paused. "Well – I guess we'll have to."

Jonathan detected the disappointment in his brother-in-law's voice. "How about lunch today, can you get away?" Jonathan asked.

"Sure, I have today off anyway. Where do you want to meet?"

"You choose the place, buddy."

"How about BJ's?" Tanner suggested.

"Great. See you at noon, OK?"

"Sounds good. By the way Jonathan, why are you going to London?"

"It's a long story Tanner; I'll fill you in at lunch, OK?"

"Thanks, Jonathan, I'll see you at noon."

Tanner put down the phone and reached for his laptop. Scrolling through its pages, he wondered if the months of tedious research, programming, math formulas and a $76 million 'paper' victory were going to be the easy part. Tanner now had less than six hours to finalize his sales pitch to the richest man he knew - and trusted. Convincing Jonathan that it would be prudent to invest a quarter of a million dollars in lottery tickets was going to be a task at which Tanner was far less skilled.

Over the years that Tanner had known him, Jonathan had made many large investments, but only after very careful scrutiny. One of the questions that would surely be raised was the amount of money Tanner himself would be willing to invest. Tanner had already determined that he would put up all his current cash assets of $25,000 to demonstrate his confidence in his plan. Now it was time to outline his presentation.

Tanner arrived at the restaurant at noon to find Jonathan already seated in a booth towards the rear of the dining room. He looked trim and tall as he stood up to shake Tanner's hand.

"You're looking good Jonathan – Hey, thanks for meeting me for lunch."

"It's been a while since we've done this, huh?" Jonathan exclaimed, shaking Tanner's hand and giving him a gentle slap on the shoulder. The waitress appeared, introduced herself and took their drink order. Jonathan ordered an ice tea, Tanner, a 'Nutty Brunette' ale.

"Carolyn wants to have you two over for dinner in a couple of weeks after I get back," Jonathan said. "She sends her love."

"I'm curious, what's your trip to London all about?" Tanner asked.

"I'm looking into an investment in a commercial property trust. London real estate, especially commercial property is doing really well and it looks like it will for some time. You know me - go the source and check it out, so that's what I'm doing."

Tanner quickly decided on his introduction.

"What if I told you that I've been looking into a company here in this country that has some great potential to make an investor very wealthy, very quickly?"

Jonathan leaned forward slightly. "I would say that coming from you and knowing how your brain works, I would definitely want to hear more about it. What's the name of the company?"

"The California SuperLotto."

Tanner smiled slightly as he uttered the words.

"And how does one invest?" Jonathan asked as a skeptical expression crossed his face.

"You invest by buying 250,000 lottery tickets – specific combinations of numbers that I select, using my formulas and my proprietary software." Tanner's answer was simple and firm.

"You're serious aren't you?" Jonathan said in an equally serious tone.

Tanner leaned forward and lowered his voice slightly.

"Jonathan, you are the only person except Sandy that knows about this little project of mine. You might think I'm crazy, but let me show you something."

Pulling a folded piece of paper from his shirt pocket, he unfolded it and placed it on the table, sliding it over to Jonathan.

"Over the last two years, I've made a study of the lottery, specifically SuperLotto Plus. I've come to the conclusion that by analyzing the patterns of lottery numbers, using analytic software programs that I have written – it is possible to win SuperLotto, assuming one has the funds to cover a sufficiently large base of number combinations. After refining these formulas, I produced a list of 250,000 lottery combinations and tested them last night for the first time, on paper - and one of my generated number combinations was the winner."

Tanner pointed to the top of the paper showing the official winning number from the California Lottery website.

"The jackpot was $76 million. Here is a photocopy of page 184 of my list of 250,000 combinations that I picked. Can you read the number I highlighted in yellow?"

Jonathan compared the numbers. "16-22-23-34-47-8, no doubt about it, they match. How did you do this?"

"You know me, I study numbers. I'm in the business of numbers. One thing that has always intrigued me is observing certain number patterns that often develop in random number games like the lottery or the roulette wheel."

"I remember once in Vegas," Jonathan recalled, "I played roulette for a while at a table where several people were playing the number 24 and everything around it. It was strange how many times it paid off."

"Well, that's a small example of obvious number patterns that often appear. In SuperLotto, the number 14, for example, has appeared 15 times in my database as the Mega number, while the number 22 has only come up once. So, I wrote a computer program that assigns a higher priority to numbers like 14," Tanner explained.

Jonathan seemed impressed but skeptical. "But, even if several numbers have a more consistent track record, still the game is random and your picks could lose, right?"

"True," Tanner agreed, "there is no guarantee with randomly selected numbers, but if you use the best analysis and cover the largest number of possible combinations, your chances can vastly improve. And, by the way, I have written several software programs that help me spot many patterns within SuperLotto data that are NOT easy to recognize; like pairings of numbers, calculating and comparing the totals of winning combinations, odd numbers versus even, not to mention putting all of this data together to produce a quarter of a million combinations without a single duplication."

"So, let me ask you this," Jonathan said, leaning forward, "could you create this result a second time?"

"I'm pretty sure that I can," Tanner said with conviction.

"So what is your plan?" Jonathan asked.

"My plan," Tanner said with a smile, "is to convince you to finance the actual purchase of 250,000 lottery tickets and split the jackpot with me. I'll do the analysis, I'll create the list, I'll organize the purchases of the tickets and you claim the winning ticket."

Jonathan pondered. "How would you physically purchase that many tickets? Wouldn't it take weeks?"

"I'm glad you asked that question, Jonathan because logistically this is probably the trickiest part of the plan. It will take teamwork to purchase this quantity of tickets because we only have three or four days between lottery draws. Each lottery play slip has spaces for five different number combinations. We will fill out all of the play slips in advance; then, each person on our team will take their tickets to various lottery outlets and purchase about 500 tickets each day from Sunday thru Wednesday, the evening of the draw. It will take a lot of organization - and work."

Jonathan seemed to be satisfied with that part of the plan.

"I'll hire and train each one of them and I'll foot the bill for that part of the plan. I'm liquid for $25,000, and I'm willing to risk it if you are. So, tell me, Jonathan, what do you say?"

"What time frame are we talking about?" Jonathan asked.

"I'm not sure; many factors are involved. The hiring and training period for the team would take a few weeks. We would want to run all the numbers only when the jackpot grows large enough to be interesting and hope that there is no winner while we make the final preparations. Probably within the next six to twelve weeks - if we start now. And there is one more thing I should tell you. The secondary prize in the SuperLotto game yesterday was $38,000. It goes to the person who picks the five main numbers, but misses the Mega number." Tanner pointed to the number on the list in front of Jonathan, "Last night I picked that one too."

Jonathan Googled the California Lottery website and showed the screen to Tanner. "The jackpot is now up to 79 million," Jonathan said.

"This would be the perfect time to do it if we had everything in place," Tanner said. "but this jackpot will no doubt be won soon and another one will start at 7 million dollars."

Jonathan put down his phone and looked thoughtfully at Tanner.

"I've got to admit that the whole idea intrigues me," he said, taking the first bite of his lunch. "What can you tell me about the programs that you've written to do this?"

Tanner smiled. "That's really the key Jonathan. The software allows me to add a number of filters to isolate any emerging or existing patterns. I've been writing similar types of programs for years as an analyst, so it comes as second nature to me. It was just a matter of customizing them for this particular purpose."

"But when you detect these patterns, what do you do with them?" asked Jonathan. Tanner could sense the rising enthusiasm in Jonathan's inquiry.

"It's complicated, but I worked for over a year writing and testing a program that translates various patterns into number combinations. Of course, these number combinations are interpreted into the 5 number sets of the lottery from 1 to 47. Then I combine all of these number sets with the Mega numbers that I choose from 1 to 27. The program generates as many number sets as I request."

As their lunch conversation continued, Jonathan began to think that this unusual proposition would be more of an adventurous gamble than a serious business investment. But the fact that Tanner was willing to put his own skin in the game convinced him that he MUST be a part of it. A loss of $250,000 would not be a crushing blow to Jonathan, who as an astute businessman had taken his share of business losses. The fact that Tanner would risk his own $25,000 spoke volumes to Jonathan. Tanner had always been the cautious one, the conservative investor, and now this idea that they could actually win the lottery was a vision Jonathan could not resist.

"Normally I would turn an idea like this down flat," Jonathan said, dangling Tanner's printout from his fingers. "but I'm so impressed with your idea that I'm going to make a proposition. You said that you could do this again, is that right?"

Tanner shook his head confidently, "Yes, I'm confident that I could do this again."

"Could you do it the day after tomorrow?" Jonathan asked.

"For the next draw?" Tanner asked.

Quickly analyzing the time frame, Tanner's expression turned serious.

"Yes, I would have to make a few alterations, and then run the numbers through my programs again, but I could generate the necessary combinations by Saturday's draw."

Jonathan smiled. "That's what I wanted to hear. If you pick another winning number Saturday, I'll bankroll this whole deal whenever you think the time is right." Jonathan held out his hand.

"Deal?"

"It's a deal!" Tanner exclaimed, grasping his brother-in-law's hand firmly.

"Of course, you DO understand that I will have to convince Carolyn that I'm making a rational decision – buying a quarter million lottery tickets. I've been making fun of her for years whenever she buys a single ticket."

"Ouch!" Tanner exclaimed. "That's going to take some doing."

"Well, I think we'll be OK. She trusts me," Jonathan said. "I think."

After lunch, the two men decided to go back to Tanner's condo to continue the planning and to let Sandy in on the news. It was decided that Tanner would start immediately adjusting and rerunning his programs in preparation for the Saturday evening lottery draw. Jonathan would stay in touch with Tanner and check in with him from London on Saturday after 8 p.m., which would be 4 a.m. on Sunday morning for Jonathan. If the results were positive, Jonathan would arrange to have $250,000 deposited in a joint account that they would set up.

The task of buying a quarter of a million lottery tickets was the problem with which Tanner was most concerned. Who would they use to form their team? Since lottery tickets cannot be purchased with credit or debit cards, the handling of that much cash could be a problem. Who could they trust? They also needed to procure 50,000 lottery play slips and pre-fill each of them with five picks from Tanner's massive database. Each of these tasks was formidable.

One possibility discussed was that of visiting dozens of the local lottery retailers and asking for large amounts of play slips for their lottery 'club' – and asking how the retailer would handle the purchase of 500 or more lottery tickets for their 'club.' Would they have the personnel to handle such a purchase? With good planning, arrangements could be made for each of the lottery retailers to bring in extra help for the day to handle the quantity of ticket processing. Perhaps they could be convinced to process thousands of lottery slips if a bonus was offered to the manager or owner of the store as an incentive. If enough retailers could be set up in advance to provide this extra service, perhaps only a small team could accomplish the task.

The planning session was winding down when Sandy returned from her shift at 4 o'clock. Seeing her brother sitting on the couch as she entered the front door, Sandy knew that Tanner's plan had been successful.

"Hi Jonathan," Sandy exclaimed as she crossed the room to give her brother a hug.

"Nice to see you Sis," Jonathan responded.

"So you guys kept this big secret for two years from your favorite brother!" Jonathan laughed.

Sandy walked towards the kitchen.

"Tanner swore me to secrecy, Jonathan. I wanted to tell you, but the time had to be right. Do you guys want a beer?"

The response was unanimous.

"So, what's the plan?" Sandy asked as she returned with the beer.

"I'm going to run the numbers again for Saturday's SuperLotto," Tanner explained, "and if we get a hit – as I'm certain we will – Jonathan has agreed to fund a real run at it when the time and jackpot size is right."

"In that case, I would like to propose a toast," Sandy said, passing out the cold bottles of beer. "Here's to the next big winners of SuperLotto – Here's to us!"

"Here's to us!" Jonathan and Tanner exclaimed in tandem as the three tapped their bottles together.

As soon as Jonathan left to finish preparing for his trip to London, Tanner began his process of setting up his programs. It had to be perfect, just like Wednesday's win. He entered a new set of numbers from the previous drawing, then ran the program again, from top to bottom. The program took three hours. Then, Tanner took the revised data and ran the program which actually assigned lottery combination numbers, based on the revised data. It was midnight by the time the numbers were generated.

"Perfect," Tanner exclaimed, "time to print these out and we're done for the day."

It was Tanner's habit to print hard copies of his work. It was easy to reference and could serve as a backup if the data was ever lost.

It had been an extraordinary day. Looking back Tanner was pleased with not only the day's outcome but the entire year. Today was the day that all of his hard work had fallen into place. Finally, he permitted himself to tell someone of his plan. Jonathan saw the plan and was so impressed that he was ready to risk a small fortune on Tanner's math and programming skills. Everything was now in place for Saturday. Tonight his slumber would be sweet.

* * *

Mario Gutierrez lifted the last of the heavy cases of beer into the cooler and slid them into place. Wiping his brow, he lingered momentarily at the open door, enjoying the cold air blowing across his face. It was a warm day and the chilled breeze was refreshing. As the young man stood there thinking about all the jobs he had over the last few months, a smile of satisfaction crept across his face. Most of them were low skill jobs lasting a few days, usually involving digging or painting, but this job would be different, he promised himself. Although this was only his fourth day, Mario loved his new job. His boss, Mr. Trung, treated him with respect - not as a day laborer, but as a man. His kindness toward Mario inspired the young man to work hard and do the best job possible. Closing the door to the cooler, he heard Mr. Trung call his name.

"Mario, please come!"

The man motioned to Mario to step behind the counter. There were few customers in the store and Mr. Trung wanted to continue training him to use the cash register and help customers. He was happy to oblige. Mr. Trung, a small Vietnamese man, was equally happy with his recent hire since many of his customers were Hispanic and Mario spoke better English and Spanish than he did. The young man was quickly gaining confidence behind the counter.

Although his new job outlook was positive, Mario's foolhardy decision to steal money from 'Fat Man' Flores had recently brought on recurring nightmares. His fear about the million dollars that he had buried in the desert was becoming obsessive. What would he do? Over and over, the young man played out various scenarios in his head. Should he retrieve the money and try to smuggle it back to Flores? Perhaps, he thought, he could recover the money, store it in an airport locker, or storage facility, and just mail the key to Carlos. This was probably the best plan so far, but would it free him from the death sentence imposed upon him by Flores?

In one of his nightmares, Mario stood at the door of Carlos Flores' compound, holding the duffle bag full of cash. After handing the money to his former boss, Carlos reached inside his jacket and pulled out a chrome pistol.

"I cannot tolerate disloyalty among my people," he said, cocking the pistol and pointing it at Mario's head. As the gun discharged, Mario saw a shower of stars, like fireworks exploding deep in his head. He convulsed, twisted, and then woke up perspiring. No, this plan was not one he would use.

Chapter 5

The Lottery Team

Tanner woke early on Friday morning to make breakfast for Sandy. She had been working hard lately and he was feeling somewhat neglectful. As a couple, they always had great fun together, but lately Tanner's focus had distracted his attention from Sandy. He was determined not to fall into that trap. Whipping up a nice breakfast for Sandy would be a nice gesture, he thought. And so it was that Sandy awoke to the smell of freshly brewed coffee.

"Wow, it smells good in here!" she said, standing at the edge of the kitchen, barefoot in her pajamas.

Tanner poured Sandy a cup of coffee and brought it to her.

"Here you go babe; hot coffee brewed with love."

"This is nice. What else is going on over here?" she said, examining the cluttered kitchen while sipping the hot coffee.

"I've just finished a nice waffle for you," Tanner said while scooping out fresh strawberries into a small bowl.

"And over here, we have some scrambled eggs and ham, hash brown potatoes and sourdough toast, my dear."

Tanner took her hand and guided her to the table and began setting out the hot breakfast. He sensed that Sandy was touched by his little gesture, and that made him feel good.

"This is so sweet of you, Tanner. Thank you."

"I just wanted to show you that you're still the most important thing in my life. I've been distracted, or should I say, consumed, by this project, but I never want you to feel you come second in my life."

Sandy kissed Tanner on the cheek and grabbed his hand. "Thank you for letting me know that. And thank you for making me feel so special this morning, you did a great job on breakfast; it looks wonderful."

"Speaking of breakfast!"

Tanner bolted towards the kitchen counter just in time to save the toast from burning. "I love dark toast," he laughed, juggling the hot slices in his hands. "Ow! Ow! Ow!" Tanner yelped, gingerly transporting the toast to the table.

"You are such a goof, Tanner," Sandy laughed as she watched her husband fumble with the toast.

"Come here my little chef."

Pulling Tanner towards her, she stood and wrapped her arms around his neck and kissed him softly. "Let's put breakfast on hold for a while and go back to the bedroom," Sandy suggested.

Tanner stood motionless as Sandy playfully undid the buttons on his shirt.

"The eggs are going to get cold," he said.

"But something else is getting very warm," she whispered.

Tanner didn't waste any time moving from the kitchen to the bedroom, hand-in-hand with Sandy. Breakfast had been a great success.

***

Later that day Tanner found himself at a local liquor store, which was the most active lottery center in his neighborhood. He approached the cashier with a dollar and a lottery slip. The man casually processed the slip and handed him the printed lottery ticket. There was no one in line, so he decided to ask him some questions.

"Are you the manager?"

"Yes, I am," the man said, while holding out his hand. "I'm Steve."

Tanner shook his hand and continued.

"Glad to meet you, Steve, I'm Tanner. I'm the jackpot captain of our lottery club at work. I was curious about the ability of your store to process a large amount of lottery tickets for our club?"

"How many are you talking about?" Steve asked.

"About 2,500 tickets."

"That's a lot," the manager said. "Let's see… five tickets per play slip would be 500 slips. How often would you need them? Every game?"

"Only during high jackpot games, like this week." Tanner said. "If you could get us 500 play slips in advance, we could fill them out and have them all ready to process."

The manager thought for a moment. "I would have to bring in someone for the day, just to handle the ticket terminal, but if I knew a couple of days in advance and if your play slips were all filled out, sure, we could do 2,500 tickets in a day. In fact, I would be happy to."

"Just out of curiosity," Tanner asked, "how much do you make for selling 2500 tickets?"

"Six cents per sale," the manager said, tapping out the figures on a small calculator. "So, let's see, that would be $150 dollars."

"Let me ask you this, Steve. If our club wanted to buy 10,000 tickets, would you be willing to bring in your help for two or three days in a row?"

"Sure, we could do that, but we would need to have a few days' advance notice to schedule our employees."

"How would I go about getting the play slips in advance?" Tanner asked.

"I can order them in advance and have them here for you when you are ready. It only takes a day or two to get the supplies. Just let me know when you are ready."

Tanner obtained the manager's card and cell phone number and again shook the man's hand, thanking him for his cooperation.

Pleased with the response from his first contact, Tanner visited five more lottery retailers and made similar inquiries. Each retailer was equally cooperative, agreeing to schedule extra help to process the large quantity of tickets for Tanner's "club." It was looking as if this plan could be accomplished by a team of 4 or 5 people.

Now it was time for Tanner to write one more program. Transferring the huge number of lottery number picks from Tanner's computerized list to the small play slips would be impossible manually. Tanner spent Friday evening and most of Saturday coding and configuring a program that would perfectly fill out the play slips, transferring the data to the little check boxes on each slip. In case there should be an issue, he programmed the marks to appear randomly hand drawn instead of machine printed. As a test, Tanner printed out 500 slips. After a few minutes of printing, he compared the list to the printed slips. Each one was perfect!

It was 4 p.m. when Tanner finished with his testing. Just as he started to pick up the phone to call Jonathan, the phone rang. It was Jonathan.

"Hello Tanner, how's everything going there?" Jonathan asked.

"Everything is set, Jonathan," Tanner said. "I've run all my programs again, and distilled a new list. In four hours we'll know how consistent these programs really are."

"I just had to call. I'm so pumped up that I can't sleep, and this jet lag is really killing me!"

"Well, give it 4 more hours, Jonathan and then you can sleep like a baby."

"So did you have any feedback from the lottery outlets yet?" Jonathan asked.

"Yes, really good response from a half dozen local stores. They all agreed to bring in extra help to process 2500 tickets. Most of them said up to 10,000 would be possible. And with a couple days' notice, I can get a supply of play slips from them in advance."

"How about the automated printing?" Jonathan asked. "Any success there?"

"It worked out beautifully, Jonathan! I finished the program and test printed 500 play slips today. - They all printed perfectly! - I'm going to look for another printer that holds more slips. My current printer only holds 100 slips, but I found a laser printer that prints faster and holds up to 500 sheets. That would be much quicker."

"You're amazing Tanner. Everything seems to be moving along really well. - Thanks for all of your hard work; I just wish I was there to help, but I'll call you in a few hours to get the results, OK brother?"

"OK, Jonathan, I'll talk to you at eight o'clock."

"Sure…and say hi to Sis, OK?" Jonathan added.

"Will do. Talk to you soon."

***

Sandy arrived home from an all-day nursing seminar. She was tired but excited about the upcoming highlight of their evening.

"I'm home, honey," Sandy announced as she started to unload her gear in the hallway. Tanner ran to help her.

"Welcome home, Babe," Tanner said. "How was your class?"

"It was good, I learned a lot, but my brain is so tired," she laughed.

"I just got off the phone with your brother," Tanner said. "He told me to tell you hello. He's so excited about tonight he can't sleep."

"I'm going to run and take a quick shower, OK? - We have a few hours until the lottery draw. How about letting me take you out to dinner?" - Sandy suggested.

The couple made their way to the Aloha Grill, one of their favorites, near the Huntington Beach pier. Although the crowd was starting to grow, they managed to find a table on the patio, overlooking Main Street. This was always a good place to watch the beach goers crowding the sidewalks below. The beautiful sunny afternoon made it perfect weather for a 'Rainbow,' a favorite drink served at the 'Grill'. Who could resist the colorful layers of slushy fruit flavors, rum, vodka, and schnapps? The calamari appetizer was perfect, as usual, and dinner with Sandy, like always, was a delight. Tanner relaxed, and for a little while, put out of mind the approaching lottery draw.

After dinner, they walked a short distance to the end of Main Street, and then crossed Coast Highway onto the Huntington Beach Pier. The sun was just beginning a slow descent into the fiery colored Pacific. - From their elevated view, they could see surfers, not fifty feet away, taking off on beautifully shaped summer waves. Quickly gaining momentum, they would then make their sharp turn at the bottom of the wave, riding it until it was time to kick out. - After the surfers paddled back out, the process would begin all over again. - Sandy and Tanner walked hand-in-hand to the end of the pier to see the final flickering of the setting sun.

"It's beautiful tonight isn't it?" Sandy said.

"A perfect evening," Tanner said, placing his arm around Sandy's shoulders. On the walk back to their car, Tanner checked his watch. It was 7:40 p.m.

"Come on baby; let's go see if we're going to be millionaires!" Tanner said as his pace changed into a trot.

"Beat you to the car!" Sandy said, laughing, as she pulled off her sandals and broke into a sprint.

The phone was ringing when they arrived at their condominium.

"I'll bet this is my brother," Sandy said, picking up the phone.

"Hi Jonathan," she said into the phone.

"Hi, Sandy. I'm just checking in. How's everything with you two?"

"We're good. We just got back from the beach. Tanner has been busy getting everything ready for tonight. Did he tell you about the good response he's been receiving from the little markets and lottery outlets around here?"

"He did. I'm thinking about finishing my business up here quickly and getting back there, especially if we have a win tonight!"

Sandy switched the call to speakerphone, so Tanner could talk to him while checking the game results.

"Hello Jonathan," Tanner said. "It's already 8:15, so, we should know any minute now."

Tanner refreshed the lottery web page several times until finally; the winning numbers appeared.

"Here we go, buddy!" Tanner shouted. Sandy clung to Tanner's arm as he read the results.

"In the smallest to largest order the numbers are 7-26-29-38-43-17," Tanner shouted.

"Jonathan, did you get that?"

"Yes, I got it," Jonathan said. "7-26-29-38-43-17, did we get a hit?"

"We'll soon see."

Tanner opened his data program and typed the six numbers into the search box. A few seconds later the highlighted number appeared.

"OK, it's a MATCH: 7-26-29-38-43 and 17. *That's the winning number!* - We did it again Jonathan! We have the winning number!"

Sandy screamed. Jonathan shouted euphorically, "You're a genius, Tanner! *You did it!* Woo-hoo!"

Jonathan was beside himself with excitement.

"I can't believe it, Sandy! – Sandy, can you hear me?"

"Yes, Jonathan I hear you! *Can you believe this?*" Sandy shouted.

Tanner then interrupted with an update from the results page - there was no winner that evening, thus raising the jackpot to $82 million.

"Now I know I won't be able to sleep again tonight," Jonathan exclaimed. "I've got to get back as soon as I can."

"I wish you were here now Jonathan, we could all celebrate!" - Tanner said.

"Well, it looks like I'm going to have to celebrate alone tonight."

"Get some sleep if you can buddy, and we'll talk to you soon. Let us know when we can expect you back here, OK?" - Tanner said.

"OK, guys, I'll be talking to you soon. And again, Tanner, *great job!*"

"I love you, Jonathan," Sandy said. "Take care and we'll see you soon, OK?"

As Jonathan hung up, the room went from bedlam to silence. Tanner and Sandy embraced in a state of disbelief. After several seconds of silence, Sandy was the first to speak.

"Is this a dream, or did you just select the winning lottery numbers twice in a row?"

"This is not a dream, and yes, I did. I can't believe it, but I did," Tanner said, shaking his head.

"I'm so proud of you Tanner. - I've always known that you were a smart guy, but I'm sure no one has *ever* done anything like this."

"I'm going to predict," Tanner stated, "Jonathan leaves London tomorrow on the first plane out and insists we start a real run for next Saturday's draw."

"Could we do that? I mean…would we have enough time?" Sandy asked.

Tanner thought for a moment. "We could if we started tomorrow."

"Tomorrow?" Sandy's eyes widened and her voice sounded doubtful, but then she realized Tanner was serious.

"Yes, tomorrow. At least we can start gathering the play slips we need. Even if we don't make the deadline - or if someone wins Wednesday's game - we'll be prepared for another lottery draw – on another day."

"Well, I'm ready if you are," Sandy said. "I don't have another shift for two more days, and I know I can work around that. Where do we start?"

"That's the Sandy I love."

On Sunday morning, Tanner's prediction came true. Jonathan called at 6 a.m. and announced that he was about to board a flight home. In a fifteen-minute planning session, the trio agreed that they would attempt a run for the jackpot on the following Saturday. Hopefully, the next game on Wednesday would again yield no winners. The jackpot would then grow to $85 million.

"I think we need to start immediately," Jonathan said. "The critical part is getting enough play slips and setting up the schedule with the retailers to process them."

Jonathan had already communicated with his bank, arranging to have $250,000 set aside for a cash withdrawal. While consulting with his banker, Jonathan learned of the tax consequences of a lottery jackpot if two people share the winnings. If one person claims the winning lottery ticket and later decides to share it with someone, the entire tax burden would be paid by the ticket owner. Later, Jonathan explained, the recipient's gift would be taxed again. It was important to create a contract to share the winnings. In this way, each joint winner would be liable for their own tax burden. Jonathan called his attorney that afternoon and had the agreement drawn up. If they were to win this lottery, and Jonathan was confident they would, this agreement could save millions of dollars in federal and state taxes.

Tanner, delighted to hear the plan, thanked Jonathan for his action. "We'll get that agreement signed right away," Tanner said.

"I'll pick it up and be ready to hit the street as soon as I land – and, by the way, Carolyn has agreed to help us too! She thinks we're nuts, but wants to join the fun."

After breakfast, the couple went into action. Tanner accessed the California Lottery website and printed out a list of lottery retailers in his zip code. There were 35 liquor stores and convenience stores within a 2-mile radius. He then transferred the addresses into Microsoft's 'Streets and Trips' program. Tanner and Sandy now had a route ready to follow and they were ready to start.

A Mom and Pop neighborhood market was their first stop. Tanner and Sandy introduced themselves and asked for the manager. The owner emerged and shook hands with them, introducing himself as

Robert. Sandy knew just what to say and got right to the point. She explained that they were employees of a wealthy man who, from time to time, likes to play the lottery - but in a big way. Although this man was eccentric, he was quite a nice man to work for. Since the lottery was about to go over 85 million dollars, he has become obsessed with buying 10,000 lottery tickets for this game.

"He knows that you probably have to bring in extra help to meet the deadline. He is willing to pay a bonus of $500 as a kindness for helping him. Do you think it could be done?"

The man stood silent for a few seconds, surprised at such a strange request. "I've never sold that many tickets at one time, but I guess I could. Do you want to buy these tickets for this Wednesday or next Saturday's game?"

"Next Saturday's game, assuming there is no winner on Wednesday," Sandy replied. "So you will have only Thursday, Friday, and Saturday – 3 full days. Can you do it?"

"That should be possible, it's a very quick process," Robert said.

"We'll need 2,000 play slips right away. Will that be a problem?" Sandy asked.

"Let me check to see how many I have on hand in my storeroom. I might have to order more, but that will only take a day or so."

As the store owner left to check on his supply of lottery slips, Tanner held up his hand and Sandy gave him a 'high-five.'

"This might be easier than I thought," Tanner said. "I think we should tell him that his $500 bonus will be paid in cash as soon as the printing of the 10,000 tickets is finished," Tanner suggested.

The store owner returned with a large plastic wrapped package and handed it to Sandy. "Here you go. There are 2,000 play slips here."

"Thank you so much," Sandy exclaimed. "We'll fill these out and return here on Thursday morning, so you can start processing them. Can you start at 8 a.m.?"

Robert nodded and replied, "Yes, 8 a.m. is fine. I'll have my son here in plenty of time to start running these for you. Remember that you will have to pay cash for all of the lottery tickets."

"We'll pay you in full on Thursday morning when we bring you the slips," Tanner said. "And we'll pay you the extra $500 bonus after the tickets are processed, OK?"

"Yes, thank you. That would be fine. Please tell your employer that I wish him the best of luck. I hope he wins!"

The store owner shook hands with Tanner and Sandy, thanking them again.

"Sandy, you are amazing!" Tanner said under his breath as the couple walked back to their car. "All we need are 24 more setups like this one!"

For the next two hours, Tanner and Sandy contacted four more stores and repeated the same pitch with each of the retailers. Only one was unwilling to cooperate. Three of the markets agreed to process the play slips. While only one had enough slips on hand, the others gave them what they could spare, agreeing to supply them with more in the next day or two. They carefully listed the locations for pick up and contact numbers to check on them.

After the first two hours, the couple split up and worked separately, dividing the remaining stores between them. By the end of the day, they had 10 lottery retailers ready to cooperate and collected over 10,000 play slips. It became obvious that the $500 bonus was the key to their success. Most of the retailers were confident that the processing of 10,000 tickets within a three day period would present no problem.

Jonathan called from aboard his flight at noon for a progress report. His plan was to join the pair on Monday, along with Carolyn. He would also withdraw the cash needed for purchasing the tickets on Thursday morning.

"I'm proud of you guys! By the time Carolyn and I hit the streets, you will have most of the lottery retailers signed up!" Jonathan exclaimed.

Later that afternoon, Tanner bought the new 500 sheet printer and decided to buy one extra for backup. By the end of the day he had the printers fine-tuned and ready to print 50,000 lottery slips.

***

Monday morning saw Tanner and Sandy again taking separate routes. After exhausting their first zip code list, a second zip code was routed and ready to go. By 11:30 a.m. Sandy finished her list and called Tanner. Together they found six more cooperative store owners and managers. With sixteen stores signed up, they decided to break for an early lunch and meet Jonathan, who had arrived home late the night before.

Carolyn was preparing a light lunch for them when the pair arrived.

"Where's Jonathan?" Sandy asked.

He should be here any minute. He went to do his banking and a few other errands." Carolyn replied.

Just then, Jonathan entered the front door.

"Well, I got it!" Jonathan said, holding up a slim briefcase, crammed with $250,000 in cash. "I guess this means we're serious about this plan!"

Tanner approached his brother in law and shook his hand. "It's really good to see you Jonathan, welcome back. Did you get any sleep?"

"Sleep; what's that?" Jonathan laughed. "I don't know if it's the jet lag or the excitement, but I don't think I've slept six hours in the last 3 days."

"Hi, Sis," Jonathan said, hugging Sandy. "It's good to be back. I missed you guys."

Carolyn, carrying a plate of sandwiches, insisted everyone sit down at the dining room table for a bite to eat.

"Sandy, Jonathan has told me about the great success you two are having with these lottery outlets. What are you saying to them?" Carolyn asked.

"I've been telling them that my employer is a very rich, eccentric man who likes to play the lottery in a big way, especially when the jackpot is this high. We tell them that he is willing to pay a $500 bonus to them if they can schedule the extra help to process 10,000 tickets on Thursday, Friday, and Saturday. Most of them were very cooperative."

"Besides, they have nothing to lose," Tanner added. "They get six cents for every lottery ticket they sell, which amounts to $600. Also, we pay them a $500 bonus. It's a great deal for them – they love it! And what they don't know is that one of the 25 retailers will win nearly a half million dollars - just for selling the winning ticket!"

"How are you doing with collecting lottery slips?" Jonathan inquired.

"We've collected about 10,000 so far, but the retailers have promised us they will have plenty of play slips for us by Tuesday," Sandy said.

"I think we need to assume that they will be late, or unable to get us the play slips we need to finish the printing," Jonathan said. "What do you think about sending Carolyn to another zip code, to collect as many slips as she can."

"I can do that," Carolyn said with a smile.

"That's a great idea," Tanner said, "The worst thing to happen would be to run out of slips, or not get them printed and returned to the stores in time for processing."

"It looks to me like we'll have our list of 25 retailers by the end of today," Sandy said, "But it would be a good idea to have a few extra, just in case."

"Before I forget," Jonathan said, handing an envelope to Tanner, "here is the agreement that my attorney drew up for us." Tanner opened it and quickly examined the document. "Today, we should stop by my bank and notarize this," Jonathan said.

The group finished lunch and separated into their individual routes. Tanner and Jonathan made a quick visit to the bank and signed their agreement. Carolyn traveled south, calling on her group of lottery outlets, collecting play slips as she went. With each store she visited, she used a similar pitch:

"Hello, my name is Carolyn; I'm the manager of a lottery club at our company. This week's jackpot is getting so large that our group has decided to buy 1000 tickets. Would this be a problem for you?"

Of course the store manager, happy to sell $1000 dollars in lottery tickets, would also be more than willing to gather 200 play slips for the attractive young woman. As the store manager, or owner, handed over the bundles of slips, Carolyn would say, with a big smile, "Would it be possible to get a few hundred more, just in case they decide to go bigger?" Usually, they would happily go back to the storeroom and come out with another bundle. Carolyn then thanked them and moved on to the next retailer on her list. By the end of the day, Carolyn had contacted over 20 lottery retailers and collected 14,000 play slips.

At 6 p.m. the group met back at Jonathan and Carolyn's to analyze the day's activities and refine their plan. While waiting for a pizza delivery, they turned their attention again to the play slip issue. What had been collected previously, plus the 14,000 Carolyn had just collected, amounted to 24,000 slips.

"Excellent job everyone!" Jonathan exclaimed. "Not counting Carolyn's stores, we have 21 outlets, ready to launch on Thursday morning."

"Assuming no one wins this thing on Wednesday night," Tanner reminded the group.

"Let's hope we can hold on for one more draw without a winner," Jonathan said. "But, right now we need to think about Thursday. Can you believe Carolyn's success in collecting all of these for us? I think that Carolyn can manage her group on her own, each with the potential of printing 2000 tickets each. These can be our 'ace in the hole,' in case some of the stores can't meet their goal."

Carolyn agreed. "I think that most of my contacts are capable of handling at least 2000 tickets each with no problem."

"Now, about tomorrow," Tanner said, "We need to get eight or nine more retailers on board, and we're still 26,000 slips short of our goal. Based on our results for the last two days, we should have no problem doing this by tomorrow."

"So on Wednesday, we should contact every single store to pick up the promised slips and make sure they will be ready to go full speed on Thursday morning," Sandy added.

Tanner explained to the group about the extremely tight schedule that would be necessary between Wednesday night and Thursday morning.

"I can't run my programs until I know which numbers are picked in Wednesday's game. It will take a few hours to run the programs, which means we won't be able to begin printing the play slips until around midnight. We'll need to print all night and into the next day. I've decided that tonight, I'm going to buy a third printer, and one more computer, so we'll have three printers working at the same time."

The fast approaching Wednesday night would take the collective organizational skills of all four of them, to print and organize 50,000 play slips.

Starting early Thursday morning, the team would then deliver to each outlet their 2,000 preprinted slips. Then, throughout the day Thursday, Friday and Saturday, the team would check each one of the retailer's progress. If one store had problems keeping up, a team member would pick up the play slips and transfer them to another location. All of these details would be communicated to Tanner, who would oversee the whole operation.

It had been a hectic day, and the group deserved a much-needed rest - especially Jonathan, who hadn't slept for several days. Tanner decided to put off buying the extra printer and computer until Tuesday, and the group called it a day.

On Tuesday morning, Tanner was up at 5:30. He mapped out and divided another zip code into four routes, then emailed two of the routes to Jonathan and Carolyn. The plan was to meet again at noon. With 21 outlets on their list, the plan was to expand that list to at least 30 by the end of the day. Tanner would withdraw the cash necessary to purchase the printer and fund the bonus money for the lottery retailers.

By noon, the group was back at Jonathan and Carolyn's. They had met their goal of nine more lottery outlets, plus they had collected another 5,000 slips.

"I suggest a celebratory dinner tonight at the 'Original Fish Company,' Carolyn said. "Who's with me on that?"

Everyone agreed. This restaurant was a favorite of both couples. It was often a choice for anniversaries and other special occasions - and this, they agreed, was certainly a special occasion.

After lunch the group divided again. Sandy, Jonathan, and Carolyn went back through their lists and checked on many of their outlets and collected most of the lottery slips needed.

They now had 40,000 play slips, ready for printing. They double checked with most of the owners and managers – making sure that they all were ready for the big push on Thursday morning.

After Tanner had finished his banking and purchasing of equipment, he spent the remainder of the day configuring the computers and printers. Calculating the speed and output of the printers, he determined that the printing would take no less than ten hours.

Sandy had made their dinner reservation at 7 p.m. Arriving a little early, the two couples enjoyed a cocktail on the patio.

The group was now 24 hours from Wednesday's lottery. If there was a winner, the jackpot would shrink back to seven million dollars, sadly putting all their work on hold. It could be many weeks or months before it would be worthwhile to try another attempt. But the group was optimistic, hoping for the best.

"If there is no winner tomorrow," Carolyn asked, "and we win on Saturday, what is the bottom line, Tanner?"

"Tomorrow's jackpot is $82 million. If there is no winner tomorrow, the jackpot will increase to $85 million – of course, that's the one we're after." Tanner said.

Tanner pulled an old lottery ticket from his shirt pocket and handed it to Jonathan.

"On Saturday night, Jonathan, you are going to be holding in your hand a ticket like this, but worth $85 million. Soon after that, we'll be walking into Lottery headquarters to fill out our claim form."

Jonathan examined the card, imagining how it would feel to be reading all the winning numbers. "Unbelievable," whispered

Jonathan, shaking his head. "I can't believe that we're that close," he said, gesturing with his thumb and forefinger.

"So, how much do we actually keep, if we win the 85 million?" Carolyn asked.

Tanner was quick with the figures. "We'll be taking a lump sum, somewhere between 45 to 55% of the $85 million. Let's figure 50%. That would be 42.5 million. Minus 25% automatically deducted for federal taxes, brings us to $31,875,000. Divided equally between both couples, would be $15,937,500 each."

"Well in that case, I'm ordering the lobster," exclaimed Sandy. The serious tone of the conversation was broken by laughter.

The hostess soon escorted the couples to a cozy booth. Dinner was delicious, as usual, as they enjoyed fresh salmon, lobster, and their favorite dish, calamari steak, smothered in a lovely Beurre Blanc sauce.

"So, tell me sis," Jonathan said, looking across the table at Sandy, "what are you going to do with sixteen million dollars?"

"This whole plan has come together so suddenly that I honestly have not thought much about it. I would like to help a few people I know who are struggling right now," Sandy replied.

"What about you?" she asked Jonathan.

"I'm going to pay off our mortgage and all of our debt. I can't remember what it feels like to be debt free. And of course, Carolyn and I would love to travel," Jonathan said, glancing at his wife.

"We might even open that restaurant we've talked about for years," added Carolyn. "And then there are children to think about." She gently patted Jonathan's hand.

"In that case, we better look for a bigger house," Jonathan laughed, "maybe a place down in Newport Beach, on the bay, with a dock."

"Sandy and I have wanted to go on a cruise for a long time; we've just never had the time. Maybe we'll do one of those 'around the world' cruises," Tanner said.

"We should all go together!" suggested Sandy.

"We'll book the nicest suites, go on all the tours – that would be great fun," Carolyn said excitedly. "We will probably each gain 20 pounds from all the food," she laughed.

Throughout the evening, the couples enjoyed exchanging the endless possibilities of their potential wealth. Each contributed ideas about their favorite charities and the need for finding a good money manager. The future of each of their careers was also discussed, with Sandy being the most determined to continue without any changes. Then, the discussion turned to the 'real' business of the next day's schedule.

Wednesday was the last day of coordination before the purchase of lottery tickets on Thursday. The results of Wednesday night's lottery draw would signal the start of their tightly coordinated plan. The minute the winning numbers are announced, Tanner would be first to go into action, re-calculating his programs, which would distill a fresh list of lottery numbers. But until that time, the team would complete the collection of 10,000 more lottery slips and prepare the lottery outlets for the action soon to explode on Thursday morning.

Before everyone went home, Tanner handed out a master list to each person. Every retailer was listed, including location, contact name and phone number. Everything was covered, and each one on the team knew their job. Now it was time to get some rest and mentally prepare for the next 4 days.

***

Wednesday seemed to fly by quickly as the group scattered and made contact with the lottery retailers on their lists. They were easily able to collect the remaining 10,000 play slips. Carolyn made contact with most of the thirty participating stores on her list. Each of them assured her that they were ready to begin processing her tickets on Thursday morning.

By 6 p.m. the group was finished and met back at Tanner and Sandy's to watch the lottery results at 7:57 p.m.

At 8:15 the results of the lottery appeared online, along with the good news that there had been NO winner. It was as if a starting pistol had been fired. The elated group went through a ritual of hugs, high fives and congratulatory slaps on the back. The time had come for the most important part of their plan to go into motion.

Tanner went to work immediately, entering the latest winning number combination into his program. It would now be a few hours before he finished performing his magic, so Jonathan and Carolyn left to get some rest while Sandy napped on the couch.

By midnight, Tanner had finished running his programs. He woke Sandy and together they began the ten-hour process of printing the play slips. Tanner gave Jonathan and Carolyn a call and within a half hour, both couples were busily printing and organizing the play slips into separate stacks on a large table.

For several hours, the group printed steadily, and by 7 a.m., six stacks of slips, belonging to the stores on Sandy's list, had been finished. Along with each stack of tickets, an envelope containing $10,000 in cash was attached. As planned, Sandy loaded everything into the trunk of her car and was soon on her way to the first stop on her list.

Meanwhile, the printing process continued full speed. As each of the three printers spat out slip after slip, the team arranged them into piles, with corresponding lists. By noon, Jonathan and Carolyn headed out to their retailers, with cash and bundles of play slips. Tanner continued the printing job single-handedly. He had estimated that it would take around ten hours to complete the printing, and by five o'clock he made his goal.

Throughout the day, team members would return and pick up more stacks of play slips and envelopes of cash and return to their assigned route of lottery outlets. At six o'clock the stacks of slips were gone. By 9 p.m. the group finished, and then returned to review the progress of the day.

Everything, so far, had gone well. The 25 main retailers were each paid in full and were busily printing lottery tickets. The next day would be spent observing the speed of production. Everyone in the group was tired, but happy with the results of the day. Tanner commended each one and told them that they had every reason to be proud of their efforts.

"Two days from now, we will make history," Tanner exclaimed, "No one has ever done what we did today, and on Saturday night we will have 85 million reasons to celebrate!"

Although the group was exhausted, falling asleep was not easy.

***

Friday morning found each of the team members back on their routes, checking the progress of the ticket printing. Sandy was the first to find a problem with one of her retailers. The terminal that reads the play slips and prints out the lottery tickets broke down. The store manager informed Sandy that another terminal would be in place later that day. But since time was quickly slipping away, it was decided that a thousand play slips would be picked up by Carolyn and taken to one of her alternate retailers. This, of course, meant the store manager would need to refund $5,000 of the cash that he was given the day before. Although not happy about the situation, he reluctantly returned the cash. Carolyn quickly enlisted two of her retailers into processing 500 play slips each. In spite of this mishap, the balance of the day went smoothly, with many of the retailers 75% complete with their ticket orders.

Saturday was the most critical day. It was important to complete the lottery ticket printing well before the 7:45 p.m. cutoff time. Around 11 a.m., another terminal had broken down in one of Jonathan's stores, with 300 play slips yet to be processed. These were immediately transferred to another one of Carolyn's stores.

By early afternoon, the printing was finished and ready for pick up. Each of the team members made their final rounds to their retailers, picking up bundles of lottery tickets. They thanked each store owner and manager who had helped them and paid each of them their $500 cash bonus. By 6 p.m. both couples were back at Tanner and Sandy's, where they stacked all of the 250,000 lottery tickets on the dining room table.

"I've got to get a picture of this," Tanner said, retrieving his digital camera, and setting it up on the kitchen bar. Carefully framing the dining room table in his viewfinder, he motioned everyone to stand behind the table. Setting the timer on the camera, Tanner ran over to join the group, standing proudly behind the mounds of lottery tickets. After the photo had been snapped, the group erupted in spontaneous applause and cheers. Tanner opened four cold bottles of beer and handed them out to Sandy, Jonathan, and Carolyn.

"This is to the best team ever," Sandy said, raising her bottle in the air.

"And here's hoping that my $250,000 will be the best investment ever," Jonathan said, clinking his bottle lightly against Sandy's.

"Think of it," Tanner announced. "Right here, on this table, somewhere in these stacks is a lottery ticket worth 85 million dollars. Is it in this stack?"

Tanner held up a bundle of tickets, removing the attached list and reading it.

"Did 'Village Market' sell us the winning ticket? Or was it in this stack - 'Trung's Neighborhood Market?' In less than two hours, we'll know!"

"I hope it was 'King's Deli'," Carolyn said. "Mr. King was so nice to me and went out of his way to help us. How much would he win if he sold us the winning ticket?"

"The seller of the winning ticket earns a half percent, or about $425,000," Tanner said.

At precisely 7:56 p.m. the team gathered around Tanner, who, with his laptop perched on the kitchen bar, sat monitoring the California Lottery website. Jonathan paced nervously as they waited for the results to appear on the screen.

"I've never been so nervous in my life," Jonathan said, "I can't believe that we're doing this."

Tanner continually refreshed the page over and over. Twenty minutes passed, with no results. He could feel his stomach tightening and his palms starting to perspire.

"The results usually appear between 8:10 and 8:17," Tanner assured the group, instinctively checking his watch.

Sandy gently rubbed Tanner's shoulders and neck. "You okay?" she asked.

"Yeah, I'm good. This is killing me, though," Tanner said.

8:18 p.m. and still no update. Tanner refreshed the page again.

"OK, OK, OK...here we go...*we've got numbers!*" Tanner said, carefully reading the fresh information that had just appeared on the tiny screen. The group closed in around Tanner.

"What does it say?" asked Carolyn.

"OK, we've got a 2, 25, 28, 36, 44, with the bonus number of 14," Tanner exclaimed. "Write that down, quick!"

"It says there is ONE winner… the winning ticket was purchased at 'LaVonne's Market,' in Huntington Beach!"

"That's on my list!" screamed Sandy. "That's Lavonne's – not five miles from here!"

Tanner, by now, had his data program opened and typed in the numbers: 2, 25, 28, 36, 44, 14. The search lasted only a second.

'NO MATCH FOUND' flashed the search box.

"What the hell?" shouted Tanner. *"No Match?"*

"Let me give you the numbers again," Sandy said calmly:

"2, 25, 28, 36, 44, and 14"

The only other sound heard in the room was the frantic clicking of the keyboard, as Tanner retyped the winning lottery number. Hitting 'enter', the search box again flashed, and finally a number appeared.

"THAT'S IT! WE'VE GOT IT! *We've got the winning number!"* Tanner bellowed. "2, 25, 28, 36, 44, and 14!"

The room burst into emotional bedlam. Tanner and Sandy embraced. Jonathan hugged Carolyn and swung her around the room.

"I can't believe it!" Jonathan shouted, shaking his head, tears welling in his eyes. Moving across the room, Jonathan gave Tanner a bear hug. "Thank you brother," he said tearfully. "I'm so glad you talked me into this."

Tanner, fighting back tears himself, responded, "Thank you for having faith in me Jonathan. You're a gutsy guy."

"I guess we should actually make sure we have the ticket before we get too carried away," Jonathan laughed. "Let's find the stack of tickets from 'LaVonne's Market,'"

Quickly, Sandy, rummaging through the mountain of lottery tickets, found the stack of tickets marked 'LaVonne's Market.'

Dividing the pile of tickets into four bundles, the group excitedly shuffled through their stacks looking for the winning ticket.

"Just look for the bonus number 14," suggested Tanner.

"God, what if we don't have it," Jonathan said.

The shuffling went on for several minutes until Carolyn screamed.

"I've got it!" She said, holding up the ticket. All four took turns holding the ticket and inspecting it carefully, repeating the numbers over and over, until they were satisfied that they had in their possession the winning $85 million lottery ticket. Again the room erupted in shouts of excitement, congratulations, and expressions of disbelief.

Just then Sandy's phone rang.

"Hello. Yes, this is Sandy." It was Martin Sully, the owner of LaVonne's Market. "Yes Mr. Sully, I just heard… yes, I know. We are so happy and surprised!"

Her conversation was punctuated with: "OK… yes… we will…I understand…good…thank you," Sandy assured the elated man that they had the winning ticket in hand, and would soon be contacting the California Lottery Headquarters to claim their prize.

"I think he was crying," Sandy said, after hanging up. "He was so excited! I'm happy for him."

"I'm happy for us!" exclaimed Carolyn. "Can you believe that we just won 85 million dollars?"

"Sandy, break out another round of beers!" Tanner said. "It's time for Jonathan and me to sign the lottery ticket!"

Ceremoniously, Tanner handed Jonathan the ticket and a pen.

"Before Jonathan signs this ticket, I would just like to thank all of you guys for making this the best day of my life - next to marrying Sandy, that is. - But mainly, I'd like to thank my brother-in-law, who had faith in me, and because of his fearlessness, it was Jonathan that made this moment possible."

Jonathan then took the ticket, turned it over and signed his name. Handing it back to Tanner, Jonathan said, "It's your turn. Sign this and put it in your safe, and let's have a beer!" Tanner signed the ticket and shook Jonathan's hand. Again, the group applauded while Sandy handed out the bottles of beer. Tanner took the ticket back to his office, where he made some photocopies of the ticket, and then securely locked it up in his wall safe.

Both couples had previously decided to keep their lottery plan to themselves. In California, all names of lottery winners become public information, so they knew that it would be impossible to stay completely anonymous, but their method of winning, they agreed, must remain a secret.

There was no way of knowing if the store owner, Mr. Sully, would keep the group's purchase of 10,000 tickets to himself. But there was one person whose curiosity was aroused from the start – Mario Gutierrez.

Mario, the new hire at 'Trung's Neighborhood Market', thought that it was odd when Mr. Trung asked him to come early to process $10,000 worth of lottery tickets for a single customer. Over the period of two days, Mario was instructed to concentrate on entering hundreds of play slips into the store's lottery terminal, then stacking the printed lottery tickets in neat, orderly piles. Mario wondered, who it was that would buy such a great quantity of lottery tickets, and why? When Mario asked Mr. Trung about this, he was told that a man named Jonathan was hired by a very rich man to oversee the large purchase of tickets. Later, Jonathan introduced himself to Mario. He inquired about the progress of the lottery ticket printing and was relieved when Mario assured him that he was making quick progress in processing all of the slips. Jonathan then handed Mario a card with his cell phone number on it and asked him to call him if there was any problem. The next day, Mario was instructed by Mr. Trung to call Jonathan to let him know that all of the tickets were ready to be picked up. When Jonathan returned to pick up the tickets, Mario could not help but voice his curiosity.

"Do you often buy this many lottery tickets?" he asked.

"No, I didn't buy these," Jonathan said, with a laugh. "My crazy boss gave me the job of buying these for him. He likes to do things in a big way, I guess!"

"He must be a very rich man," Mario observed. "Does he ever win with such a large purchase?" He could tell that Jonathan was becoming a little uncomfortable with the young man's questions.

"I don't think he's ever won, but maybe, this time, his luck will change. To tell you the truth, I think he has more money than he has brains."

Jonathan thanked Mario, shook his hand and thanked him for his hard work. Before Jonathan left the store, Mario noticed that he had a short conversation with Mr. Trung before handing him an envelope.

***

Toward the end of their exciting evening of celebration, the couples agreed they should consult with a business attorney that Jonathan had worked with for many years. That evening Jonathan contacted him by phone and reported the good news of the lottery win. An appointment for the group to consult with him was made for the following day. Following the brief conversation, Jonathan reported to the others:

"Richard will see us tomorrow at one o'clock, at his office. His main advice right now is to keep our mouths shut, take our time, and not rush into anything, including the claiming of our winning ticket. We've got plenty of time to claim our win, but before that, we need to take a breather and talk to some professional financial advisors."

"I think that is good advice," Sandy said. "There's no rush."

"Richard Stewart is a smart, well-respected attorney," Jonathan assured them. "He specializes in business law and he's a great tax attorney. He's saved me a ton of money over the years and his advice has always been top notch."

"How about a CPA - does he have one that he works with?" asked Tanner.

"He works with several good ones," replied Jonathan. "He'll probably recommend one that specializes in this type of thing."

With an emotional day behind them, the elated group of lottery winners was ready to get some well-deserved rest. They could sleep soundly tonight, knowing that they had in their possession, locked away safely, the single winning ticket for the $85 million California SuperLotto jackpot. Tomorrow they could address the legal and financial subtleties, but tonight would be the time to dream big.

Chapter 6

Change Your Phone Numbers

Richard Stewart turned out to be an important resource for the new lottery winners. Besides being experienced, he was pragmatic.

"Friends you never thought you had; cousins that you never knew existed, will suddenly appear from nowhere, with their hands out," he cautioned. "It's uncanny. Your phone will start burning up with calls from every financial advisor, fund salesperson, and budding entrepreneur, with ideas of what to do with *your* money."

Richard's advice was to shut down every phone number they have, starting that very day.

"Change every cell phone number and home phone to an unlisted status. If you don't, your time will be squandered away, answering your phone, telling people that you are not interested in their plan, and hanging up on them. Also, change your e-mail addresses."

"Isn't there some method of remaining anonymous," Sandy asked. "Could we set up a trust? Wouldn't that keep our names out of the news?"

Richard explained that, unfortunately, in California, lottery winner's names become public record. Avoiding the onslaught of publicity by hiding behind the veil of a 'Trust', has never been successful in California. Even if one establishes a trust as an instrument to hold lottery winnings, the name of the trust director must remain public.

"I don't mind being the one to take the bullet," Jonathan said, "After all, someone has to appear at the Lottery headquarters to claim the jackpot."

"Well, that's good. I think we all know Jonathan can take the pressure," Richard said. "Plus, you're a professional investor, and when all of this dies down, others may simply assume that you've made some extremely good investments."

Jonathan laughed.

Their attorney opened a manual of California Lottery regulations and quoted from it:

"PUBLIC DISCLOSURE OF WINNER'S NAME

1. The California State Lottery Commission finds that a winner's name, the name and location of the retailer who sold the winning ticket and the amount of prize (including the gross amount and net payment, if applicable) may be public records under the California Public Records Act and, therefore, subject to public disclosure. The Lottery will not disclose personal information (e.g., age, home address, employer, phone number, etc.) without the consent of the winner unless required by law.

2. The Lottery may announce the public information identified above in any manner determined by the Director, including via the news media."

"The lottery folks try to get the most publicity out of a big win like this," Richard said, "so when Jonathan shows up with the winning ticket, they will want a public news conference. Of course, they will ask you all to be there, but that's not necessary. They will ask you how you chose your numbers, what your plans are for the money, and so on. But you don't have to answer any questions if you don't want to. Just say no to anything that makes you uncomfortable," Richard advised.

"You guys already have a joint ownership statement drawn up, which is good. So we will draw up an official 'Multiple Ownership Claim Form' to go along with this and submit both to the California Lottery people," Richard said.

"This will make it a simple disbursement procedure for them. It will be an even split after federal taxes have been withheld. Most likely each of the partners will receive around $16 million after taxes. It could be $17 million, depending on the percentages they use."

Richard explained to the group that managing that amount of money would be a full-time job. He recommended setting up a meeting with a Goldman Sachs wealth adviser he knew to be highly regarded.

"I'm telling you what I would personally do if I were in your position," Richard said. "A company like Goldman can help you manage your wealth over the long haul, with investment advice custom - tailored to your lifestyle. They specialize in handling high net worth portfolios. The adviser I have in mind only works with people with a minimum of ten million dollars in assets. After talking with him, he and his team can analyze the best possible ways to protect your money and grow it safely – and with the minimum amount of tax liability. You could never do what they do by yourself - trust me."

Jonathan looked at Tanner and Sandy. "What do you think, guys?"

"We should at least talk to him and hear his ideas," Sandy replied.

"I agree," Tanner said. "Goldman is a huge worldwide company. In fact, the company I work for does business with them. When can we get an appointment Richard?"

"You already have one," the attorney said with a grin. "I've set up a tentative appointment for tomorrow afternoon at 2 p.m. if that will work for you. Their office is in Los Angeles. I think we should all go together if that's all right with you."

Everyone agreed, and arrangements were made to meet at Richard's office the following day, at noon.

"Something else you need to decide is how to handle your careers," Richard said. "What I would recommend is that you try to keep your same routine in life and work. If you are going to make any career changes, be sure not to rush it. Sudden wealth is, in my opinion, like getting married. It's a huge change in your life, but after the first year, it starts to feel normal, so don't be hasty about making important decisions. Keep your life as normal as possible. After you claim your winnings, and after the news gets out, you might consider taking off a few weeks – an extended vacation, and then try to return to your normal routine."

After their meeting with Richard, all agreed that a slow, steady approach to their new circumstances made good sense. His counsel about taking their time, consulting with the best financial experts, and trying to resume a normal routine was just what they needed. Now it was time to put some of his good advice to work.

While returning home from their attorney's office, Carolyn made a suggestion.

"I think that we should plan a two or three-week European cruise."

Sandy, of course, agreed with the cruise idea. As an option, she suggested a Caribbean cruise.

"The other day," Jonathan added, "I was reading about an 'around the world' cruise that was 100 days long. Now that's what I call taking some serious time off!"

"And that would be a good period of time to put behind us after the news of our winning becomes public," Tanner said. "Let's grab some food and go back to our place and check out some cruises online. Hey! It's only money!"

Sandy laughed. "Tanner, I can't believe you just said that."

Everyone understood Sandy's statement. Tanner was, after all, the most conservative of the group. Every purchase or financial decision that he made was subject to scrupulous analysis. This earned him the label of 'tightwad'. Jonathan, on the other hand, was known as the 'big spender,' the one who wore the expensive clothes and drove the BMW. Tanner admired Jonathan and secretly wanted to be more like him while Jonathan always looked to Tanner as his stabilizing influence.

Later that evening, the group decided the 100-day, 'around the world' cruise would be much too long. They settled instead, on a European cruise vacation of three to four weeks. Since there were so many possibilities, it was decided they needed some expert advice.

Their research led them to the name of a highly respected cruise specialist, Don Berkebile. Don was known in the travel industry as 'Mr. Cruise', having more cruises under his belt than most other professionals. A retired Navy man, he earned the reputation of knowing more about every ship, every cruise line, and every itinerary, than anyone in the industry. A phone call to Don convinced them that this was their man. Taking note of their preferences and schedule, Don promised to do his best to organize the perfect cruise.

Within two days, Don had thoroughly sifted through every cruise possibility. Since the couples wanted to leave as soon as possible after their lottery win became public, his choice of available voyages was limited. He did, however, discover one cruise that would surely satisfy the requests of the most sophisticated traveler.

The Noordam, one of Holland America's finest 'Vista Class' ships was sailing in just 6 weeks on a 20-day European cruise. One of the special requests of the couples was that of procuring the best suites available, and the Noordam had not yet booked their two 1300 square foot 'penthouse suites'. These luxury suites were the finest in the fleet, consisting of a living room, dining room, bedroom and a private verandah complete with an outdoor Jacuzzi. Don was sure that the itinerary would also please his new clients.

Leaving from Rome's port of Civitavecchia, the 82 ton Noordam would cruise north to Livorno, Monte Carlo, Barcelona, the Isle of Mallorca, La Goulette, Tunisia. Then, the voyagers would turn east, across the Mediterranean to Sicily, and on to Naples. The second half of their itinerary would include another stop in Rome, then, on to Croatia, followed by four stops in Greece, including the Islands of

Corfu and spectacular Santorini. The final part of the voyage would take them to Ephesus, Naples and back to Rome.

Carolyn, who was informally elected by the group to be their cruise coordinator, was delighted when she heard the details of the cruise. She instantly reported the good news to the group, anxious to get their opinions on the itinerary and the $20,000 price tag per person.

Jonathan, of course, was thrilled, as was Sandy. To everyone's surprise, Tanner thought the price was a bargain and insisted that they book it quickly before the penthouse suites were taken.

"I think that tonight, a celebratory dinner is in order," Tanner declared.

Carolyn agreed and took the liberty of making reservations at 'The Original Fish Company' for the four of them.

The European cruise was not, however, the only reason for celebration that evening. Two days before, the group had met with financial advisors from Goldman Sachs, along with their attorney, to discuss financial strategies. To their surprise, Richard arrived in a limousine to transport the couples to their meeting in Los Angeles.

"Don't be surprised at this kind of treatment," Richard said in a serious tone. "Goldman believes in treating their clients and potential clients in a first-class fashion."

The meeting was about an hour long and well prepared by two of Goldman's 'wealth management specialists. They outlined in detail, their proposal for each couple. They suggested the setting up of a revocable living trust for each family. The trust, they explained, was like a container to hold all of their assets. It protected their assets from probate, in the case of death, and to a small degree, protected their privacy. As for where their money would go, the company had prepared a detailed power point presentation which was displayed for them on a huge screen, showing the breakdown of various investment ideas. A mixture of treasury bills, bond funds, equity investments and short to medium-term CDs was suggested. It was suggested that a very conservative investment strategy would be the way to start, gradually evolving into various kinds of investments in the future. Emphasis was put on growth, balanced with limited tax liability. It was clearly explained to them that the federal taxes of 25% that would be taken, right off the top of their winnings, was not the end of their tax liability. Depending on their tax bracket at the end of the year, there may be a secondary tax due. Their advisors assured them that they would work hard to minimize, or even negate that secondary tax. It was estimated that based on the proposed plan, each couple could expect a yearly income of more than one million dollars, after taxes.

It was agreed by everyone, that the Goldman presentation was impressive, and sounded like a good plan to start with. Richard advised them to think about it for a few days before making any final decisions, and offered to set up appointments with other financial experts for comparison, if needed.

The celebratory dinner at 'The Original Fish Company,' like always, was a delight. The smell of the mesquite wood, used to fire the huge broiler, which was in full view of arriving diners, made their appetites soar. A round of specialty martinis and some shrimp cocktails, followed by shrimp and scallop ceviche, was a good way to start the evening.

Carolyn brought a file folder, full of cruise information to share with the others.

"Has anyone been to the Holland America website and looked at the penthouse suite?" Carolyn asked, flipping through her stack of information.

"Tanner and I were looking at the photos and the room diagram last night. What a beautiful suite, and so huge," Sandy said.

"Listen to this," Carolyn said, dutifully reading from a cruise brochure. "Penthouse Suite - Bedroom with 1 king-size bed, oversized whirlpool bath & shower stall, living room, dining room, dressing room, pantry, 1 sofa bed for 2 persons, mini-bar refrigerator, guest powder room, floor-to-ceiling windows, private stereo system, microwave, 1,126 - 1,318 sq. ft. with verandah."

"That's almost the size of our condo, Sandy," Tanner said. "But our condominium doesn't cost two thousand dollars a day."

"Your condominium doesn't cruise all over Europe, with first class food, entertainment, stewards, chefs and bartenders," Jonathan said. "Besides, you're rich Tanner, you can afford it. Remember, it's only money."

Tanner laughed. "You're right, I am rich. So, just to show you I'm starting to adjust to my new lifestyle, I'm paying for dinner and drinks tonight."

"Wow, Tanner, you are really starting to get the hang of this new lifestyle, aren't you?" Jonathan said. "Sandy, did you hear what Tanner just said?"

Sandy laughed and affectionately patted Tanner's shoulder. "He's come a long way, and I'm proud of him."

Tanner, nearly blushing, had to laugh. But it was a strange feeling, being a sudden millionaire. He had spent so much time and energy over the last few years, working on his theories and his programming. He hadn't really thought about the 'being rich' part. Now, with the winning lottery ticket in hand, the changed circumstances were a new challenge to deal with. Thankfully, he had Sandy, who had always been his touchstone of reality. He knew that they would never be overwhelmed by their new found wealth, with no clear path to follow. Unlike the stories of how sudden wealth had shattered the lives of some lottery winners, Tanner knew that, with Sandy, their lives would only be enhanced. Tanner, like the others, was starting to get the 'big picture', and he liked what he saw.

Dinner conversation that evening was filled with plans for their European cruise. Sandy and Carolyn had researched every stop the ship would make and the tours that would be available to them. Their flight to Rome, from where the cruise would sail, would be first class, of course. They decided to arrive two days early to explore the 'Eternal City,' and an extra day at the end of the cruise. After comparing several of the finest hotels in Rome, the couples singled out the St. Regis. Based partly on the 5-star rating and the solid reviews posted on the internet travel site, 'Trip Advisor', it was decided that this stately hotel would be the perfect place to relax after their long flight, and serve as their home base for exploring Rome. To the group's delight, it was Tanner who insisted on booking two 'Couture Suites' at 3,000 Euros per night.

Jonathan brought up the subject no one had yet addressed. When would they officially claim their winning ticket?

"We have less than six weeks before our cruise, and I'm not sure how long the actual claiming process will take," Jonathan said.

"We should claim our winning ticket right away," Tanner suggested. "We have done our due diligence, we've sought out good advice, we have a financial plan - I think we're ready to claim our prize."

Everyone concurred, but who would go to the lottery headquarters, was the question? Sandy spoke up first.

"Since all of us, as a team participated in winning the prize, why not make the claim as a group? I think we should all go together."

"I think to protect our privacy, the fewer of us the better," Jonathan said. "Each photograph taken of us, means we'll have that much less privacy. Since Tanner and I have a signed contract to share the winnings, let's minimize the exposure and keep it to the two of us, is my suggestion."

After the discussion, they agreed that the next day, Tanner and Jonathan would represent the group by visiting the regional lottery offices in Santa Ana. The girls decided that while their husbands where taking care of business, a shopping day was in order, to prepare for the cruise. At the end of their delicious celebratory dinner, Tanner picked up the tab of $300.

"Chicken feed!" Tanner exclaimed, throwing down his credit card. It was a wonderful way to end an eventful day. It was good to be rich.

Chapter 7

The Claim

It was 10 a.m. when Jonathan arrived at Tanner's condo. Sandy and Carolyn had left earlier that morning for breakfast and their planned shopping trip. Tanner had everything together that they would need. The lottery ticket was carefully protected in its own large envelope. His birth certificate, the contract and the 'Multiple Ownership Claim Form' was in another folder.

"I wonder why this is making me feel so nervous?" Tanner said, as he slid into the driver's seat and snapped his seat belt buckle securely. "It's like the feeling I get when I go to the dentist; I know everything's going to be okay, I just have this strange little feeling of anxiety on the way there."

"Nothing to worry about, buddy," Jonathan said confidently. "It will actually be fun, I think."

"I'm going to let you do most of the talking, alright?" Tanner said.

"Not a problem. Just let me handle these people," Jonathan said.

The drive to the regional Lottery office in Santa Ana took only about twenty minutes. As they walked into the surprisingly small office, they saw an impressive wall mural, depicting various lottery winners. Some were posing with large, oversized checks, emblazoned with their names and enormous amounts of money.

"These are the types of photographs we want to avoid," Jonathan whispered, as they approached the receptionist. "No kidding," Tanner replied under his breath.

"Good morning gentlemen. How can I help you this morning?" the receptionist said, with a perky tone to her voice.

"Good morning," Jonathan said. "We're here to claim our winning ticket for the SuperLotto Plus drawing."

Wasting no time - Jonathan removed the ticket from the envelope and placed it on the receptionist's counter. Tanner noticed Jonathan's hand quiver slightly as he retrieved the ticket. The receptionist smiled broadly and picked it up.

"Oh, my!" she said, flipping over the ticket and examining both sides. "We wondered when this one would be claimed! May I be the first to congratulate you?" She stood to shake hands with the men.

"I'm Rita Ellis," she said in an animated voice. She seemed genuinely excited and happy to meet them.

"Hello Rita, I'm Jonathan Taylor, and this is my brother-in-law, Tanner."

"You must be so excited!" she said, carefully placing the ticket back into the large envelope.

"Let me just explain the procedure, and get the paperwork started for you. First, I'm going to make a photocopy of the ticket and make out a receipt for you. Then we'll take physical possession of it. The ticket will then be officially authenticated, which usually takes only a few days. May I ask which one of you is the owner of the ticket?"

"We are equal owners. Here is a notarized agreement that we have made," Jonathan said, handing the form to the receptionist.

"I see," she said, perusing the document. "And I see you have both signed the back of the ticket."

"Yes, that's correct," Jonathan replied.

"Now, if I could ask you please for some identification, such as your driver's license, and hopefully you have brought your birth certificates. We will also need your social security numbers."

Jonathan and Tanner, being well prepared, handed everything requested over to the receptionist.

"Let me have you get started filling out these claim forms, and while you're doing that I'm going to let Harold Johnson, our office supervisor, know that you are here. He'll be the one in charge of getting you through the claiming procedure. He will explain your options and answer any questions you might have."

She handed each of them a clipboard with a couple of pages of forms attached to each one and left the room, disappearing down a long hallway.

"I think she just disappeared with our $85 million lottery ticket in her hand," Tanner whispered.

Jonathan laughed. "I hope she *really does* work here."

Rita, the receptionist was gone only a few minutes, and then returned in the company of a balding, older gentleman. Tanner and Jonathan were finished filling out the forms and returned them to the receptionist.

"Harold, these are the claimants that I told you about. This is Mr. Jonathan Taylor," she said, motioning towards Jonathan, "and this is Mr. Tanner Riley, his co-claimant."

"I'm very glad to meet both of you," he said, shaking their hands vigorously. "I'm Harold Johnson. It's always an exciting day for us when big winners, such as yourselves, come into our office. May I be the second person to officially say congratulations to both of you! Rita has the best job here in our office, since she is always the first to meet the various lottery winners."

"Well, thank you," Tanner replied. "We really can't believe that we're actually here."

"That seems to be the case with many lottery winners, coming to grips with the reality of their win. But let me assure you that you are indeed the apparent winners of the Super-Lotto Plus jackpot of $85 million! I only use the word 'apparent winners' because the ticket must be authenticated by our experts in Sacramento. I've scanned the ticket personally, and our computer reads it as a winner – and the only winner at that!"

"So what is our next step?" Jonathan asked.

"We'll go back to my office where I'll get some more information from you, and then we will set up an appointment for you at your convenience. You are welcome to bring along anyone you'd like to assist and advise you, such as your attorney, if you'd like. We'll sign all the necessary documents, and then make arrangements to transfer the funds to your accounts. Does that sound easy enough?" Harold was smiling.

"That sounds very easy," Jonathan responded.

"All right then, can I get you gentlemen some coffee or maybe a soft drink before we go back to my office?"

Tanner and Jonathan declined the offer. Soon they were in Harold Johnson's office, which, like the lobby entrance, was festooned with photos of past lottery winners, all holding checks that were six feet long.

Tanner couldn't resist the question. "Harold, if I may ask – are all winners of large jackpots obligated to pose for these pictures?"

"No, not at all," Harold said with a smile. Of course we always request that our winners have a few photos taken for the media, but that is your choice. It seems to be a long standing tradition with most lotteries. Some of our winners have taken their own personal family photos holding the big check, but not making the photos available to the media."

"Jonathan and I – and our wives are concerned about maintaining as much privacy as we can. I'm sure you can understand that," Tanner said.

"Yes, very much so," the supervisor replied.

Harold next took out a form from his desk drawer and dated it in the right hand corner.

"Now, gentlemen, let's get to some of the details we need from you to process your claim. First, have you determined how you would like the disbursement of the funds to be set up? You probably know that you have basically two choices for payment. The first is an annualized payment over a period of 20 years. The second choice is a single payment made now. Are you familiar with how this is done?"

"Yes, we are familiar with the options and both families have agreed to the lump sum payment instead of the 20 year payout," Jonathan said.

"Do you have an attorney, and have you consulted with him and/or with other advisors to choose this method of payment?" Harold asked.

"We do and we have," Tanner answered.

"Very well," Harold said. "I will have you fill out this brief form that basically affirms your agreement to a single payment option. But before you fill those out, we must legally describe to you the actual figures involved in your case."

Harold reached across his desk for some printouts that had just finished printing. He handed each of the two men a copy.

"As you can see, the lump sum payout is substantially lower than the $85 million that you won. You would receive 53% of the $85 million, which is as you see on line 11 to be $45,050,000. Federal taxes of 25% will be deducted, which are shown on line 13 as $11,262,500 bringing the total lump sum payment to $33,787,500. Line 15 shows the lump sum payment to each of the two claimants to be $16,893,750. Now, looking at the annualized payment section, you see the payments to be made to you over a 20 year period?"

"Yes, I see," Tanner said.

"Your payment for your first year, before taxes, would be $2,125,000," Harold explained, "which as you can see in column 1 is 2.5% of the jackpot. Each year the percentage and the payment grow a little larger. For example, year number two payment would be 2.7% of the jackpot, or $2,295,000. By year 7, for example, your yearly payment would be 3.2% or $2,720,000. And year 15 would be 4%, or $3,400,000. Does that all make sense to you?"

"We fully understand the payment structure, and have decided to take the lump sum payment," Jonathan stated.

"All right, then you will need to state your decision on this document that I have given you and sign it in the presence of a notary, which we will have available at our next meeting, so don't sign it yet. Now, the next thing is the transference of funds. Have you set up an account to handle these funds?"

Harold took two more printouts from the printer and handed them to Tanner and Jonathan.

"We have both met with Goldman Sachs and have begun setting up accounts with them. All we need to do is finish signing papers with them sometime this week," Tanner said.

"Very good," Harold said. "It's obvious that you have done your homework, which makes my job much easier. If you would, please fill in all of the information about the banking arrangements that you have made, including the page that describes any trusts that you will be using. Please bring that information with you to our next meeting also. So that brings us to our next decision, when would you gentlemen like to set up our meeting? I suggest you give yourselves and your financial and legal people time to complete all of the necessary paperwork."

"How about a week from now?" Jonathan said. "Next Thursday morning?"

"That is fine with me," Tanner said.

"All right then, we will see you next Thursday at 10 a.m., here at our office. Until then, if you have any questions at all, just call me at this number and I will do my best to help you," Harold said, handing his business card to both men.

On the way out, Rita, the receptionist met them and returned all of their identification documents in a manila envelope. The two men were soon on the road back home again, relieved that everything had gone so smoothly.

After returning from her shopping trip with Carolyn, Sandy spent the remainder of the day salvaging her work schedule. She decided to try resuming her normal work schedule for the next six weeks, and then take a leave of absence for one more month for her cruise vacation. Although the last two weeks had been truly the most exciting in her life, and the lottery win like an amazing dream, Sandy was looking forward to getting back to the routine she had grown to love – nursing.

Sandy discovered a good thing about herself in these last two weeks. Despite having won this enormous amount of money - which would no doubt establish her as the wealthiest nurse in California - Sandy was eager to return to nursing. Her career decision had never been for the money – and that realization brought her a great deal of satisfaction. Her next shift, she was informed would be during the upcoming weekend. She decided that now was the time to let her co-workers know about the lottery win before they heard it from someone else, or on the news.

Tanner also had some decisions to make. He was proud of Sandy's decision to return to nursing as soon as possible. He had always known that Sandy had found in her career the perfect conduit for expressing her love of people. But what about himself, he wondered? Tanner enjoyed his career, but did he love it enough to return to the daily routine of statistics, after suddenly becoming a multimillionaire? His confliction, however, was soon tempered by his conservatism. Remembering the advice of his attorney, he realized he would be best served by sticking to a career in which he excelled, and which gave him the sense of stability that he needed. Sandy applauded Tanner's decision, and felt that both, returning to their careers, would help keep them grounded. Tanner arranged to return to work the following Monday, and like Sandy, he too decided to inform his staff and friends of his lottery windfall.

Jonathan and Carolyn's career decisions came easier than that of most big lottery winners. Jonathan's career was that of an investor. Thankfully, he had just made the best investment of his life, thanks to Tanner. Nothing substantial in Jonathan's life would change. He had always been a self-driven, highly motivated entrepreneur.

Working from their home office, his staff consisted of himself and Carolyn. Together, they run 'Taylor & Randall', their investment company. The name incorporates both Jonathan's family name and Carolyn's maiden name. Carolyn, a very savvy organizer is, in reality, the lifeblood of their investment business. She very effectively multi-tasks the jobs of bookkeeper, travel coordinator, property manager and secretary.

Now, with Taylor & Randall about to be infused with $17 million, investment opportunities, previously out of reach for the couple, were looking deliciously feasible. Carolyn was interested in buying apartment buildings in local Orange County. Jonathan planned on returning soon to the United Kingdom, resuming his investment strategy in overseas commercial property. In terms of lifestyle and career changes, Jonathan and Carolyn were probably the least affected; they would just continue doing what they did best.

Chapter 8

The Road to Redemption

Mario Gutierrez forced himself to walk at a normal pace, while scanning the huge parking lot for the right vehicle to steal. The main thing was to not look suspicious, he reminded himself. Carrying a bright red 'Macy's' shopping bag, any casual observer in the parking lot that morning would have assumed the young man was walking to his car. After reaching the end of the parking lot, he headed back between the long aisles of cars towards the Mall. Now, he would appear to be a customer on his way to return an item, or someone who forgot where his car was parked. He knew this part wouldn't take long, and he was correct. After a few minutes of walking, his target appeared. A white Toyota pickup sat parked at the far end of the parking lot. The ignition keys dangled from the steering column. Why people leave keys dangling in the ignition was always a mystery to Mario. It was one of life's constants – a phenomenon that always worked in his favor. As he expected, the doors were locked. Mario reached inside the 'Macy's' bag and pulled out an old spark plug. After checking the area, the young man, with a quick sidearm throw, chucked the spark plug through the passenger's side window. The quick action punched out a two inch hole in the glass, with almost no sound at all. The window easily gave way to a couple of smacks of his fist, wrapped in a towel. Looking around, he quickly unlocked the door and slid inside. Within two minutes, Mario and the Toyota exited the parking lot and headed toward John Wayne Airport.

Driving around the loop of the airport terminal, Mario pulled into a parking structure entrance. Approaching the parking booth, the young man pushed the green knob and took the parking ticket that ejected from the machine. He then drove to the farthest, darkest corner of the structure where he discovered a similar small truck parked. He knew most vehicles were parked in this lot for several days. Hopefully, it would be many days before the owner discovered that his license plate had been swapped with a stolen plate. Mario parked the Toyota and deftly exchanged the license plates of the two trucks. It was an old trick, but it gave him a certain sense of security while driving a stolen vehicle for any length of time. Upon exiting the parking structure, Mario returned the parking ticket to the attendant.

"Sorry man, I pulled into the wrong lot."

"No problem buddy, it happens all the time," the gray haired attendant laughed, took the ticket and raised the exit barrier.

Exiting the airport area, Mario made the transition to the 55 freeway north and within a few minutes he made another transition east on 91. Soon he would be leaving California behind, while eastbound on Interstate 10 towards Tucson, Arizona.

Mario's plan for this trip was not spontaneous; he had thought about this long and hard. For months, he had done nothing to change his difficult situation, and it was starting to drive him crazy. Even if this risky trip to Arizona in a stolen truck turned out to be a big mistake, at least, he was doing *something*. His new job at Trung's Market was as close to a "normal" life as Mario had experienced in a long time. Now, he thought, if he could somehow return the stolen money, and make amends with Carlos Flores, he could attain the true freedom he longed for.

But now he needed to focus. This trip would summon all the street-smart skills Mario possessed. He glanced at the speedometer, then at the rear view mirror, to make sure he was maintaining a low profile in the eastbound traffic.

Seven hours later he reached Tucson. Mario glanced at his watch; it was 6:45 p.m. Topping off his tank with gas, he walked back into the little mini-mart for his change, and to pick up a few candy bars. He needed a sugar jolt after the non-stop road trip.

"Looks like rain," Mario said, glancing out at the darkening skyline.

"Yeah, a big one is coming in," the cashier said as he handed back the young man's change.

"I'm heading over on 86; how's the highway?"

"It should be fine, but if this rain gets bad, there could be a washout or two. You headed for the Indian reservation?" the cashier asked.

"Yeah, I've got a friend over in Sells I haven't seen in over a year," Mario said.

"Well, be careful out there."

Mario thanked the man and returned to the truck just as the rain started. He un-wrapped a Snickers bar and devoured it in three bites, before resuming the last 90 mile leg of his trip. A few minutes later, Mario turned onto Highway 86, the primary east – west route through the Tohono O'odham Indian Nation. This reservation, the size of the state of Connecticut, straddles Arizona and the Mexican state of Sonora; in effect, a country within two countries. While working with Carlos Flores, Mario became very familiar with this area. It became his main route in, and most importantly, out of the United States. He had learned this route from Flores himself, who used these goat paths to haul tons of marijuana and cocaine into the U.S., and millions of dollars of drug money back to the cartel. Flores developed crucial relationships with tribe members who were able to freely travel within the confines of their tribal lands. With the help of these insiders, the area of the reservation was an easier place to operate for Mario. For over a year, he worked this area regularly, under the noses of the U. S. Border patrol, whose resources here were spread thin. The Sinaloa cartel occasionally worked these same trails, but concentrated their "trade" of drugs and the human trafficking of illegals more to the west, around Lukeville, and east, in the Nogales area.

The rain was now intense. Mario turned the windshield wipers up to their fastest setting. The broken window on the passenger side of the truck didn't help the situation. Cold air, laden with the smell of the pungent creosote bushes, filled the cab. Mario turned the heater and defroster on full blast. An hour later, arriving at the tiny town of Sells, the young man turned the stolen truck due south towards the Mexican border. Thirty miles later, Mario was where he needed to be. The area had undergone few changes, and Mario easily found the cutoff, leading to a large landfill. Soon, the pleasant desert aroma of the wet creosote bushes and mesquite trees changed to that of a noxious garbage dump. He parked his truck and turned off the lights and the engine. All he could hear was the pounding rain on the roof of the truck. He hadn't seen a car for half an hour. The rain was proving to be his perfect cover. After donning a light jacket and retrieving a small military-type folding shovel, Mario walked a hundred feet up a shallow hillside, to a huge mesquite bush. Two feet from the base of the Mesquite, he began digging in the mud. He recalled how difficult the digging was on the day he buried the money. Thankfully, on this evening, the retrieval was almost effortless. Within a few minutes, he felt the shovel hit the canvas bag. He continued digging around the bag until he uncovered the thick strap of the duffle bag. Pulling on the strap with all his might, the bag popped free. Mario ran back down the hill and threw the shovel in the back of the truck and the duffle bag through the broken window. Once inside, he turned on the interior light and unzipped the bag. Inside, wrapped in clear plastic and duct tape, were ten bundles of cash. They each contained exactly one thousand $100 bills.

By 11 p.m. Mario had retraced his route and was back in Tucson. Checking into a Motel 6, the young man took a hot shower to warm up, and fell into a deep sleep while watching the news.

The next morning Mario awoke to a bright, sunlit day. The rain had passed, and the Cicadas could be heard buzzing in the nearby mesquite as the temperature in Tucson began to rise. It was time to get moving. His next step was important. After a quick breakfast, Mario drove up and down the boulevards of Tucson, looking for a storage facility. The first one he found was on 22nd Street, called 'Extra Space Storage.' Mario drove in and parked. He was shown the smallest storage locker available, a five by five cubicle. After filling out the paperwork, the young man paid $225 cash, in advance, for a 12 month rental. Securing the bag of cash in the unit with a large padlock, Mario had only one more thing to do before heading back to California. In an envelope, prepared with the address of Carlos Flores, he placed the key, taped to a card, and mailed it from a Tucson post office. In a separate letter, Mario enclosed the gate code to the storage facility and a letter to Carlos, a message he hoped would temper the big man's wrath:

'Mr. Carlos Flores,

With the most respect, I write this letter of contrition to you sir. I have made the biggest mistake I could possibly make by stealing from you, my friend. You have always been good to me and I am sorry for my actions. In another envelope, I have sent you a key to a storage locker in Tucson, Arizona. Every dollar of the money I stole from you can be found there. The address is 8100 E. 22nd St. It is locker #312. Carlos, I beg of you to forgive my mistake and allow me to have another life, here in the United States.

Humbly, your servant and friend,

Mario.'

Chapter 9

The Check

Tanner opened the heavy glass door and with a sweeping motion of his hand said to Jonathan:

"After you, my millionaire friend."

Jonathan smiled. Tanner confided that he again had that nervous, "visit to the dentist" feeling in the pit of his stomach, as they arrived at the lottery offices for their meeting with lottery officials. Richard, their attorney, had just called and was due to arrive in the next 2 minutes.

Rita, the receptionist stood and walked over to the two men, extending her hand. "Good morning, gentlemen," she said, in a bubbly voice, as she shook their hands. "I saw you coming in from the parking lot and I already notified Mr. Johnson that you've arrived. Can I get you some coffee?"

Both men declined. "No thanks, I've had my limit for the day," Jonathan laughed.

Just then, Harold Johnson, the office supervisor, entered the lobby. Simultaneously, the men's attorney, Richard Stewart entered.

"Well, it looks like everyone is here," Tanner said, as all were formally introduced and shook hands.

The three men were escorted by Harold to a conference room, where they sat down at a large oval table. Within a minute, they were joined by another member of the lottery headquarters staff, whom Harold introduced as Milo Hudson, another senior staff member of the regional office. Milo carried a folder that was full of documents and started spreading them out on the table.

"Gentlemen," Harold began, "speaking for Milo, myself, and the entire staff, I would like to again congratulate you on your lottery win of $85 million, one of the largest in SuperLotto history!"

Milo then held up a page, with the letterhead of the California Lottery at the top for all to see.

"You will be happy to know your ticket was determined to be 100% authentic by officials in Sacramento. Here is your copy of this notification," Milo said, sliding 3 copies of the notification across the desk, toward their attorney.

Thus began the hour-long exchange, signing and photocopying dozens of documents. Thanks to Richard, everything was in perfect order, legally and financially. The meeting ended with the presentation of two checks, one for each of the family trusts, in the amount of $16,893,750.

Harold, smiling broadly, stood up and applauded the winners. Then, Milo and Richard joined in the applause. Tanner was speechless. Looking at Jonathan, who appeared to be tearing up, Tanner then thanked everyone on behalf of both families.

"If it would be all right," Harold said, "we have a couple of media people waiting out in our lobby. Would you mind a couple of photographs and a brief interview?"

Tanner and Jonathan looked at each other. They knew this part was inevitable. They agreed to the interview, with the stipulation that it would be brief. Milo escorted four reporters back to the conference room and introduced them to Tanner and Jonathan.

"Can you tell us how your life will change after winning $85 million?" one reporter asked. A microphone flew from out of nowhere into Tanner's face.

"I hope that it only changes for the good," Tanner answered. "I mean, you hear stories of how winning the lottery has ruined people's lives, and we certainly don't want that to happen. My wife and I are going to do everything in our power to stay the same as we are now."

"Are you going to quit your job?" another reporter asked.

"No – both of us and our wives have careers that we enjoy, and we intend to pursue these in as normal fashion as possible," Jonathan said.

"How did you choose your winning lottery numbers?"

"I'm going to let Tanner answer that one," Jonathan chuckled, motioning with his hand towards his friend. Tanner looked surprised, his mind racing to come up with a simple answer to the question.

"I, uh, just did what everybody else does," Tanner said, shrugging his shoulders. "I have a few favorite numbers that I play from time to time, and this time – it seemed to work." Tanner's sheepish response generated a gentle wave of laughter throughout the room.

The interview and photo session went on for another 15 minutes, until finally, Jonathan and Tanner politely excused themselves and made their way out of the building to their car. After thanking Richard for his valuable assistance on their behalf, the men were soon on their way back home, each with their $16.8 million check in hand. It had been, to say the least, a surreal morning, but it was now comfortably behind them.

That evening, the TV news reports touted the group's lottery win as 'the second largest SuperLotto prize ever won in California.' The following day, the newspapers carried similar articles, including one that read: "Two Huntington Beach couples share $85 million SuperLotto jackpot." Another article interviewed Martin Sully, the owner of LaVonne's Market, who was awarded $425,000 for selling the winning ticket. Some articles and news reports contained photographs of Tanner and Jonathan, making them feel somewhat uneasy, but following the advice of their attorney, all of their phone numbers were changed, limiting any unwanted phone calls.

The weeks that followed were very busy for the new lottery winners. Gradually they forced themselves to resume a normal pace of life and work. Tanner was greeted by a very excited group of co-workers upon his return. Upon learning of Tanner's fortune, most were very happy for him, although some questioned why he made the decision to continue working. He tried to remain philosophical about the reasons. His work had always brought him a measure of happiness and satisfaction – so why change things now? Many big winners had been known to retire and devote themselves to a life of self-indulgence, but Tanner explained that he and Sandy didn't want to become a slave to their money. Instead, they were determined to continue living the life they had built for themselves and had always enjoyed.

Sandy expressed similar sentiments to her workmates. Some assumed that she would be leaving her nursing career behind. Those who knew her best, however, were not surprised to see her return to her work with renewed energy.

Children's Hospital of Orange County, or 'Choc,' as it is commonly called, was where Sandy found great satisfaction, working in the busy world of pediatric care. The young patients of all ages loved Sandy, and she enjoyed her work with the children and their parents.

Within this environment, she would, occasionally meet frantic parents who, with a sick or injured child, were without money or medical insurance. Although not part of her duties, Sandy worked tirelessly to help these desperate families find the right channels for assistance. Steadily, Sandy developed a personal network of benevolent doctors, nurses and technicians to assist families with the financial burdens that come with a serious illness or injury. It was not unusual for her to gather donations from the nursing staff for a family in need. Now, with her new financial circumstances, she looked forward to doing even more for those needing a helping hand.

Chapter 10

A Drug Runner's Epiphany

It was nearly time for Mario to leave for work. The young man, having finished his breakfast, was dutifully brushing his teeth while watching the morning news, when an interview with the latest California lottery winners flashed on the screen. He stood motionless, toothbrush in mouth, as he listened to the report. Mario instantly recognized one of the lottery winners. It was the man who recently bought 10,000 tickets at Trung's Market. He rinsed out his mouth and dried off his hands and face, then quickly rummaged through his pile of miscellaneous papers that he kept on his desk. Finding the card he was looking for, he examined it closer. He saw the name 'Jonathan' scribbled on the card, followed by a local phone number. He remembered the man asked to be contacted if there were any problems with the processing of the lottery tickets.

Mario quickly turned on his computer and did a Google search of 'Jonathan Taylor.' In a couple of minutes, Mario found a few interesting things about Jonathan. His Facebook page proved most revealing, showing not only a photo of Jonathan and his wife, but also information about his investment company 'Taylor and Randall.' On the same Facebook page, Mario also found a photograph of the other lottery winner appearing with Jonathan, described as his brother-in-law, Tanner Riley and Sandy his wife.

Returning to the TV, Mario rewound the news program with his DVR and played it again in its entirety. The co-winner of the lottery, Jonathan's brother-in-law, Tanner Riley, was asked by the reporter how he chose his lucky numbers. He stated: "I have a few favorite numbers that I play from time – to - time, and this time – it seemed to work." Mario became intrigued by the man's glaring lie. *"Just a few numbers?"* he repeated to himself sharply, in the otherwise empty apartment. Mario then recalled precisely the words told to him a few weeks prior to this news report. When asked by Mario if the man often bought so many tickets, Jonathan told him:

"No, I didn't buy these. My boss gave me the job of buying these for him. He likes to do things in a big way."

Mario was not easily fooled. Clearly Jonathan had lied about purchasing the tickets for his employer. This could only mean the two men also purchased an equal amount of tickets at LaVonne's Market – the reported seller of the winning ticket. Why, Mario wondered, would two men risk $20,000 on lottery tickets? How many more tickets may these men have purchased? Mario was determined to find out more about Tanner Riley, but he was running late for work and this would have to wait until later.

***

'Tanner Riley'- Mario typed the name into the search box. It was late evening and he could feel the effects of a busy day starting to catch up with him. His curiosity had driven him to hurry through his work to return home to research this mystery man - Tanner Riley and his brother-in-law, Jonathan. The last name was common enough, but "Tanner," the first name was unique, hopefully unusual enough to make this search a little easier. Within a few minutes, Mario had an interesting background dossier on Mr. Riley. He worked in the city of Irvine at 'Pacific States Indemnity, Inc.' - a large Orange County insurance company. His job description was that of an actuarial analyst. "An actuarial analyst?" he muttered in an undertone.

"Let us see what this man is all about," he said as he Google searched the phrase: "what does an actuarial analyst do?"

The screen came alive with the various duties and skills needed to become an actuary. After scanning several articles, Mario's eyes were drawn to one particular statement:

"What does an actuary do? Actuaries apply financial and statistical theories to solve real business problems. In effect, they use their skills in math and statistics to create theoretical models of the world around them."

The epiphany came quickly and intuitively. Mario realized he had stumbled upon a potential gold mine. There was no question that this man, Tanner Riley and his brother-in-law Jonathan, had used some type of mathematical formula to win the lottery. He wondered how this could be possible. But how it was done was for now, an irrelevant question. Mario knew that it had been done, for he had personally printed each of the 10,000 tickets. The real question was, what would he do with this information? Could this man's secret, become Mario's ticket to freedom from "Fat Man" Flores?

"I must learn more about Tanner Riley."

Chapter 11

Rewards

Embarkation is the term describing passengers loading themselves and their belongings onto a ship. This is perhaps one of the most exciting phases of a luxury cruise. Especially for someone who has never experienced shipboard travel.

Tanner and Jonathan, mesmerized by the size and stateliness of the 82 ton Noordam, stood motionless on the quay, looking upward at the magnificent ship. Their driver, having delivered the two couples to Rome's port of Civitavecchia, busied himself with unloading the luggage onto a cart. Carolyn and Sandy joined their husbands in admiring the tall vessel. "How many decks does it have?" Jonathan asked.

Carolyn replied, "I think it has eleven passenger decks. She looks like a skyscraper from here, doesn't she?"

Jonathan returned to assist the driver with the final small pieces of luggage, when a ship's porter arrived to take the luggage to the loading area.

"I can hardly wait to see our cabin," Sandy said excitedly.

After Carolyn tipped the driver 100 Euros, the couples followed the porter to the luggage staging area, where everything was checked and tagged. They were then directed to the inside terminal where a large crowd of passengers had gathered for the check-in procedure. One of the Holland American staff members led them directly to the line marked: Suite Check-in, where only a few passengers stood in line to check in, be photographed, assigned a photo ID and room keys.

"I like this line better." Jonathan muttered in an undertone.

"No kidding." Tanner laughed, as he looked out at the sea of passengers standing in several roped-off lines. "Kind of like flying first class, huh?"

Tanner and Sandy had never flown first class until three days prior, when they boarded their flight at Orange County Airport to Rome. The new millionaires had always flown like most everyone else – cheap coach - The type of tickets which were non-refundable. Tanner always wondered, while passing through the first class section, who these first class passengers were. They seemed so comfortable in their wide, plush, leather seats, perusing newspapers, and chatting on their cell phones. To Tanner, it was like a cultural ritual: The common folk, pass slowly through the privileged realm of the VIPs, who, having enjoyed the perk of advanced boarding, observe the poor devils, as they slog their way to their cramped little seats in the back of the airplane.

The lottery windfall had certainly changed all of that. On the flight to Rome, the couples enjoyed first class service, advanced boarding, friendly, helpful flight attendants, wine, and great food. The leg room was wonderfully spacious, and the wide seats made the 13 hour flight so very comfortable.

Arriving in Rome, the couples enjoyed the luxury of a limousine pick-up and a quick trip through the bustling city to the Hotel Saint Regis. There they basked in the luxury of the impeccably decorated Couture Suites, each over 1200 square feet. Their two day tour, although abbreviated, included the Vatican, the Forum, and a wonderful guided tour of the Coliseum, Trevi Fountain and the Spanish Steps. But where the Spanish Steps end, the Via Condotti begins, and so it was no coincidence that Sandy and Carolyn planned this location as the last part of their visit.

Via Condotti is the Rodeo Drive of Rome, lined with Italy's finest luxury shopping venues. The shops of Christian Dior, Bruno Magli, Prada, Gucci, Tiffany's, Cartier, Georgio Armani, Valentino,

Salvatore Ferragamo, among others, became fair game for the girls. After an hour of shopping, Tanner and Jonathan found a comfortable bar to recharge at, while they let the girls continue their shopping adventure on their own. The first leg of their trip proved to be a wonderful first class experience, but now it was time to board the Noordam for the next part of their adventure.

The boarding process was smooth and quick. A smartly uniformed staff member led them up a sparkling glass elevator to their suites on deck 7.

There are 2 'Pinnacle Suites' on the Noordam - PS 7045 and PS 7046. These are by far the finest accommodations available on any cruise ship. Those who occupy them, they would soon discover, become the fascination of many of the other passengers. Carolyn had been insistent that these special suites must be available to both couples before booking the cruise, and now, upon entering the magnificent rooms, they knew that this was a small fortune well spent. Each of the suites had its own butler. Roberto, would be at the service of Tanner and Sandy in suite 7046, and Daniel, in suite 7045.

Roberto escorted the Riley's through the 1300 square-foot suite as if he were the owner, proudly pointing out the unique amenities of this floating palace. Opening the sliding glass doors, he motioned the couple to step out onto their private teak-decked veranda.

"As you can see, you will have plenty of room to relax, sunbathe and enjoy your private Jacuzzi."

"Oh, I love this." Sandy exclaimed, sitting down on one of the deck lounges. "I think it would be wonderful to arrange a small cocktail and hors d'oeuvres party out here, don't you think, Tanner?"

Roberto was quick to offer to make the arrangements for them. He then escorted them through the suite, pointing out the beautiful artwork, mahogany furniture, the Waterford crystal and Rosenthal china. He explained that pressing and laundry services were complimentary, and that he would be happy to arrange it for them as needed. In addition, he outlined the special services such as hors d'oeuvres served before dinner, complimentary corsages and boutonnieres provided for all formal nights. The couples would also enjoy priority dining and seating requests, daily breakfast and high tea service at 3 p.m. every day. Before leaving, Roberto insisted that if they were in need of anything, he would be at their service.

"My goal", Roberto said, "is to make this the most memorable vacation that you have ever enjoyed. Do you have any questions?"

Tanner reached for Roberto's hand, shook it and slipped 100 Euros into it.

"You have been more than helpful, Roberto, thank you for making us feel at home."

Tanner knew that this crew member would be very important to insure a smooth cruise. His "green handshake" sent a message that he appreciated good service and was generous to those who provided it. Roberto graciously thanked the couple and excused himself.

"Wow." Tanner exclaimed, gazing at Sandy.

"Wow indeed - It's like we won the lottery or something!" Sandy laughed.

Tanner walked over and pulled Sandy close to him.

"Are you happy baby?"

Sandy looked up at Tanner and planted a firm kiss on his lips. "I'm very happy. This has been like a dream, and we're just getting started."

Tanner smiled and agreed. "Yes, we are, and this evening we're sailing off to Livorno! Now let's take a look at Jonathan and Carolyn's suite."

The door to suite 7045 was open and Daniel, their butler, was just leaving as Tanner and Sandy arrived, hand in hand, like high school sweethearts.

"How do you two like your new digs for the next three weeks?" asked Jonathan.

"Carolyn, these suites are terrific!" Tanner said, hugging his sister-in-law appreciatively.

"We've got to thank you for scoring these beautiful suites for us. You've done an awesome job putting this trip together."

"I think this is a luxury we deserve, considering what we've accomplished together in the last few weeks, don't you?" Carolyn asked.

Sandy agreed and told them that she had arranged an in-suite dinner party for the first evening of their cruise.

"And later tonight, I want to get Tanner up to the disco!"

***

It was 5:30 a.m. when Tanner's alarm coaxed him to consciousness, reminding him of his plan to watch the ship's docking at the Port of Livorno. Leaving Sandy snoozing comfortably, Tanner dressed and made his way to the Promenade deck. There, one could easily walk the perimeter of the entire ship and observe the arrival. The sun was just peeking from below the horizon as the huge ship slowly slipped into the bustling harbor. Below, he could see the taxis and shuttles maneuvering their way through the harbor area, preparing to transport the arriving passengers. Tanner ducked into one of the ship's buffets for a cup of coffee, and then returned to the deck to watch the crew expertly ease the grand ship into her berth.

This early morning ritual, Tanner noticed, was the experience of only a handful of guests on-board. These hardy passengers engaged in walking and jogging around the promenade deck in the early morning glow.

It would be another half hour before disembarking would begin, so Tanner returned to his suite, where Sandy, already dressed, was putting the final touches on her makeup.

"Did you have a nice view of the harbor?" she asked.

"Yes, it's beautiful out there," Tanner answered, "I watched the crew dock this monster of a ship. Very impressive."

"My brother and Carolyn are almost ready for breakfast. Are you hungry?"

"I've had a cup of coffee, but I could use a good breakfast," Tanner replied. "When is our driver arriving?"

"We're scheduled to leave at 8 a.m.," Sandy said, "but there's plenty of time for breakfast if we leave now."

The couples bypassed the regular tours normally provided by the cruise line in favor of a private van and local tour guide. Their private tour would take them into the city of Florence to experience some of the world's greatest art and culture. After a buffet breakfast, the couples disembarked, to meet their driver and guide.

They were met by a sharply dressed young man standing next to a large new Mercedes V class passenger van.

"Good morning, ladies and gentlemen, or as the Italians say, 'buon giorno'. I am Cristofano your guide for today."

"Buon giorno, Cristofano, I'm Jonathan. This is my wife Carolyn, my sister Sandy, and my brother-in-law Tanner."

Cristofano shook hands with each, and then directed the group's attention to his driver, a slim built man in his fifties, busily polishing the sparkling van with a soft towel.

"Our driver today is Lorenzo. We are very lucky to have this man at our service today. Lorenzo is the most experienced driver of our company and very familiar with our destinations today. I always feel safe with Lorenzo at the wheel, and I know you will enjoy the safest trip today as we travel to Florence."

Lorenzo responded by tipping his cap and waving to the group. Opening the doors of the Mercedes, both the driver and the guide assisted the group into the van and helped stow their belongings.

The day turned out to be glorious, and so did the well-planned itinerary. The group made their way to Florence, through the heart of Tuscany and into the magnificent Florentine capital. On this V.I.P tour, expertly guided by Cristofano, there were no lines of tourists to wade through. Avoiding most of the crowds, they enjoyed the priceless art and rich culture embodied at the Academia Gallery. The most impressive highlight was Michelangelo's 17 foot statue of David. Cristofano was an amazing resource of knowledge, guiding his guests through the Academia and on to the Palazzo Vecchio. Next, the group continued to the Uffizi Gallery, described by Cristofano as one of the most important art museums in the world. There, they were introduced to the works of Leonardo daVinci, Botticelli, and of course, Michelangelo.

After a brief snack and a well-deserved rest, the couples were taken to the Church of Santa Croce, where the tomb of Michelangelo was located. Behind the church, a group of Franciscan monks operate a leather-working factory and artisan's school. Their itinerary included a tour of the factory and school, which proved to be fascinating. Tanner found the most beautiful leather coat he had ever seen. At $800, it became the favorite memento of the trip. Jonathan was impressed by a uniquely crafted leather briefcase, while the girls each found several purses for themselves and as gifts to friends and family. The Franciscans gladly packed and arranged for the shipment of the items home for the convenience of the group.

Shopping around the area of Santa Croce was without equal, and was only halted by the reminder from Chrisofano that it was time to start their return to the ship.

"But now," Cristofano said, "we have saved the best for last." A smile swept across the young guide's face as he described the next destination.

"No doubt while traveling in this beautiful country of ours, you have had a chance to enjoy Gelato, yes?"

"Yes," the group responded. "We love Gelato!" Sandy exclaimed.

"Excellent!" Cristofano said. "But now you will enjoy the best Gelato in all of Italy...Vivaldi's!"

An expression of pride resounded in Cristofano's voice as he described the upcoming Gelato experience.

"I have tasted it all, my friends. Vivaldi's is world famous for its quality Gelato. But today, you will be the judges!"

"Bring on the Gelato!" the group evoked. "Bring on the Gelato."

Although their visit to Vivaldi's was a brief one, it was nonetheless a wonderful view of the cuisine and culture of the Florentine people. Each one in the group marveled at their particular choice of flavors served. Each one also agreed with Christofano, that this was the most delicious Gelato they have experienced while in Italy.

"This is such a nice way to end the day!" Sandy said enthusiastically as they walked back toward the car. "This is an incredibly beautiful city."

Reaching the car and turning for a last look at picturesque storefronts, Sandy spotted two young children standing outside of Vivaldi's. The boy looked about six or seven and the girl about five - probably brother and sister. Sandy excused herself, and then walked briskly back towards the children.

"Vuoi qualche gelato?" Sandy asked.

The young boy responded hesitatingly, "No, va bene, grazie."

But the look on their young faces belied their response. Sandy insisted, and walked to the front door of Vivaldi's and motioned for the children to follow her. The young girl looked at her older brother and smiled. Opening the door the children walked in and stood motionless at the counter, staring in wonder at the colorful choices.

"Which one do you like?" Sandy asked with a sweeping gesture.

"Cioccolato," the young girl answered.

"Fragola," the older brother said.

Sandy ordered a double scoop for each and handed it to them. With grateful expressions on their faces, they eagerly took charge of the delicious cones.

"Grazie bella signora," they expressed to Sandy.

"Enjoy," Sandy said, patting the children on the head, and started back towards the car.

"Ciao...goodbye." she shouted as she stepped into the waiting car.

"Such sweet children," Carolyn said as they drove away.

"Very sweet children," Sandy agreed.

"What a nice treat for them." Tanner said admiringly to his wife.

Sandy smiled. "And a very nice treat for me too."

As the group headed back to the ship, most of them nodded off to sleep as the Mercedes wound its way through the Tuscan countryside. The ambiance of Florence, the impressive art and history, and of course, the incredible Gelato, made an indelible memory. But now it was time to return to their ship and prepare for the next day's adventure in Monte Carlo.

The Noordam slowed to a snail's pace as it approached the harbor of Monte Carlo. It was a few minutes before sunrise. Having sailed through the night with its passenger's fast asleep, her crew now made preparations to enter the harbor and dock at Nouvelle Digue de Monaco, the main passenger liner pier of Monte Carlo.

Jonathan joined Tanner on this morning of arrival. They stood on the Promenade deck, sipping hot coffee and enjoying the golden glow of the approaching sunrise. The glimmering lights of the principality of Monaco started to fade as the cool morning met the heat of a rising sun.

"What a magnificent city," Jonathan said, taking in the scene below. Across the harbor, hundreds of luxury yachts packed the harbor. The street traffic was starting to build along the narrow streets above the harbor. These same streets become the race course of world class formula racers each May as the famous Grand Prix of Monaco grips the tiny city of Monte Carlo. Averaging over 140 mph, the world's fastest Formula drivers take on the 78 laps of the most dangerous race course in existence.

"How long until we dock?" Jonathan asked.

"It shouldn't be long," Tanner said, pointing at the long dock jutting out from the yacht harbor. "We'll probably be docking over there."

They decided to move to the port side of the Noordam to get a better view, and within 20 minutes the giant ship was tied snugly to the dock.

After reuniting with the girls and enjoying a leisurely breakfast, the plan for the day was set into motion. The girls hired a car and driver to take them on a tour of the city and to some of the "hot" shopping areas. Tanner and Jonathan, as planned, would go to the main casino and check out the gambling action. They arranged to meet back at the ship by 5 p.m. - in time for the 6 p.m. sail-away. The evening was scheduled as "formal" night for the passengers of the Noordam, to the delight of Sandy and Carolyn. They planned to shop extensively for this evening.

As Carolyn and Sandy climbed into the car, Tanner kissed Sandy goodbye and suggested that they get together later in the day for drinks. "Give us a call and we'll figure out a good place to meet, OK?" Sandy said. "Maybe we'll meet you at the casino." Jonathan checked his cell phone and dialed Carolyn's number to make sure his international cell phone plan was working. Carolyn's phone rang loudly from inside her purse. "All systems are go!" Jonathan shouted into his phone, laughing. The driver closed the door and the girls waved goodbye.

Tanner and Jonathan decided to walk into the town and do some sightseeing along the way to Casino Monte Carlo.

Table gambling for casino visitors was to open at 2 p.m., leaving plenty of time explore Monte Carlo on foot.

Tanner and Jonathan could not help but be impressed with the magnificent yacht harbor. Hundreds of impeccably maintained yachts could be seen moored, or berthed throughout the private marinas. A couple mega-yachts could be seen with helicopters perched on their aft decks. Ferraris and Bentleys were parked throughout the area.

"You know, Tanner," Jonathan noted, "We've just won a major lottery, winning millions of dollars. Looking around this city is starting to make me feel poor."

"I know what you mean," Tanner said. "Imagine the money it would take to buy and maintain these yachts."

After walking around the arching road that surrounds the harbor, they decided to find their way to the highest point. Upon inquiring, they were given directions to the oldest section of the city called Monaco-ville. Perched on Le Rocher, a huge rock outcropping overlooking the city, this is the location of the Prince of Monaco's palace. It was well worth the climb, they agreed, as they admired the panoramic view of the city and harbor.

"I'm glad I brought my camera," Jonathan said as he photographed the beautiful vista below them. "Have you ever seen water so blue?"

After walking around Monaco-Ville for an hour or so, the men decided to relax and have a drink. They came upon a small bar with an inviting outside eating area. There, the men found a table with a panoramic view of the harbor. Jonathan ordered a glass of red wine, while Tanner ordered a beer. Holding his bottle of beer in the air, Tanner quipped – "I wonder what the poor people are doing."

Chapter 12

What the Poor People are Doing

Mario Gutierrez parked the borrowed car in the alley behind the 16th Street condominiums. It was midnight, and the Huntington Beach neighborhood appeared quiet. The young man checked his watch and exited the car quietly, gently nudging the door closed. Walking to a side gate of the condominium, Mario found it unlocked and entered the property. In a few feet he stopped at the side door to the garage. Pulling a small flat tool from his inside jacket pocket, the young man deftly jammed and twisted the door jamb mechanism until the door popped open, undamaged, with barely a sound. Simultaneously, a small red light on an alarm panel next to him began to blink, and Mario could see the crawling display reading: "Alarm will engage in 60 seconds – Enter Code." After prying off the cover of the panel and ripping out one of the connectors inside, the blinking light stopped. Mario sighed heavily, and then carefully replaced the alarm cover, thankful that he had seen the alarm panel in time. The last thing he needed, he thought, was to be arrested for burglarizing a rich man's home and be deported back to Mexico.

Once safely inside, he began to feel more confident. He had a mission to accomplish and many questions to answer. But he knew it must be done quickly.

Flicking on a small flashlight, the garage became faintly illuminated, revealing two automobiles, a couple of bicycles and a surfboard. Walking around the perimeter of the garage, Mario noticed two new cardboard boxes which had been taped closed. Being careful not to damage the tape, he opened one of the boxes just enough to pull out a handful of the box's contents.

"Mr. Riley, I think you bought more than just a few lottery tickets." Mario whispered under his breath, holding up a bundle of lottery tickets. Taking his cell phone from his pocket, the young man snapped several photos of the tickets and the boxes. Noticing that all the tickets were each dated the same, he pulled loose a few of the tickets and stuffed them into his pocket. Then, after carefully returning the tickets to the box, Mario pressed the tape down smoothly, leaving no trace that the contents had been disturbed.

Stealthily, Mario made his way from the garage, into the residence, looking for clues that would explain the hoard of lottery tickets he had just discovered. Examining the downstairs and finding nothing noteworthy, the young man made his way upstairs, opening the door to a small office. Three computers and three printers sat prominently in one corner of the room. Moving closer to examine them, Mario noticed a small stack of Lottery play slips lying on the desk, next to the printers. Opening the paper tray of one of the printers, he could see a stack of blank lottery play slips. It became obvious that thousands of game slips were processed on these printers. Mario took another photo before turning his attention to the other side of the office. On the wall, he caught sight of an unusually ornate framed painting. Instinctively, he moved across the room to the painting. Pulling on the edge of the gilded frame, the painting swung open, revealing a wall safe. Examining it closer with his flashlight, he decided to try a trick he learned early in his career. Many people, Mario knew, often leave their safe only partially locked. If the combination is three or four numbers, they will sometimes lock the safe when finished - then dial all of the opening combination, with the exception of the last number, making it easier to open next time. He carefully moved the dial clockwise, slowly, until he heard a slight "click" in the dead quietness of the room. Mario smiled to himself as opened the safe. Burning with curiosity, he removed the entire contents of the safe, including a laptop and a leather binder. Placing them on a nearby table, he quickly examined them under the faint beam of his flashlight. He had already been inside the home too long. It was time to leave, but this could be the most important clue of the night. The young man opened a large leather binder to discover a financial plan from Goldman Sachs. Anxious to leave, Mario snapped several photos of the report, before returning it and the laptop to the safe. Hopefully, Mario thought, the Riley's would return home without the slightest suspicion that the secret of the lottery tickets had been discovered. The broken alarm system would prompt a service call, but nothing else. It was time to leave as quietly as he had arrived.

***

Looking at his watch, Jonathan reminded Tanner the Casino would open shortly. The men paid for their drinks and headed down the hill towards the famous Monte Carlo Casino. Although the casino opens earlier in the day for tours and slot machine play, the table games, such as craps and roulette are not open until 2:00 p.m. Tanner and Jonathan each had a thousand dollars set aside for gambling, and roulette was the game they both intended to play.

Approaching the twin towered casino's grand entrance, the first thing the men noticed were the beautiful cars parked nearby. Apparently, the regulars like to arrive in style for their gaming forays - leaving the keys to their Rolls Royce's, Ferrari's, Bentley's and Lamborghini's, in the hands of the valets. The surrounding plaza was a dazzling display of extreme wealth. Manicured gardens and hedge lined lawns, punctuated by marble and tile walkways framed the classic architecture of the centuries-old buildings. The casino itself, however, was the magnificent centerpiece. Approaching the entrance, the men were impressed with its ambiance. This place was, without a doubt, designed to impress, if not to intimidate the visitor.

The pair passed through the vaulted atrium area and into the casino itself, where the table games had just opened for play. The true high rollers were not to be found in this part of the casino, however. The VIP clients did their gambling in private rooms, elsewhere in the casino.

Spotting a roulette table with only three players, the men moved in, seating themselves. After buying in, it was only a matter of minutes until a lovely waitress appeared, to take their drink order.

"A dry Martini," Tanner said. "In a deep champagne goblet."

"Oui, Monsieur."

"Just a moment. - Three measures of Gordon's, one of vodka, half a measure of Kina Lillet. Shake it very well until it's ice-cold, then add a large slice of lemon-peel. Got it?"

"Oui, Monsieur."

"A scotch on the rocks for me, please," Jonathan said.

The waitress smiled, recorded their drink order and wished them good luck as she walked away.

"What in the world was the drink you just ordered?" asked Jonathan.

"A Vesper Martini - made famous by James Bond in 'Casino Royale.'"

Jonathan shook his head and chuckled as he placed his first bets, scattering his chips around the table, $10 here and $10 there. The Croupier launched the roulette ball with flair as the patrons finished positioning their chips.

Tanner placed $500 on one vertical row and $500 on the next vertical row, covering all but twelve numbers. "Last bet," called out the Croupier as the white ball bounced around the wheel and finally settled into the 24 slot. "24." Called out the Croupier.

"Dang." Jonathan exclaimed, realizing that he had just missed the winning number by a space or two. Tanner was paid 2 to 1 on the first column, while losing $500 on the second column. The play had just netted him $500.

"What did you just do?" Jonathan laughed, while Tanner smugly scooped up his $1500.

"I'm playing the dozens," Tanner said, while placing two more piles of chips on both outside rows of a dozen numbers, "just like James Bond did in Casino Royale."

Jonathan scratched his head. "I don't remember that scene."

"It wasn't in the movie, it was in the book. Bond played the dozens, like this, for several spins and eventually won several hundred thousand francs." Tanner explained.

Jonathan loaded up number 14 and everything around it with $5 chips. Meanwhile, the Croupier announced: "No more bets."

The ivory ball bounced and tittled across the grooves and frets of the wheel, finally settling into number 21 red, catching Tanner's row of 12, netting him another $500. Jonathan won $80 on number 21, but lost $200 on his other positions.

"That was brutal." Jonathan said, placing another smattering of chips around the number 14.

"Why 14?" Tanner asked.

"14 was the bonus number on our lottery win." Jonathan laughed. "Maybe it will hit again."

"No more bets." The croupier announced.

Again the roulette ball bounced around the wheel until finally settling on the number 14. Jonathan shouted "Hey hey - 14!" as the croupier pushed Jonathan's winning chips across the table.

The croupier slid another pile of chips across the table towards Tanner.

"I love this game!"

The pair played on for another hour, with Jonathan breaking even and Tanner ahead by $3,000 dollars. Their play was interrupted when Jonathan's phone rang. It was Carolyn and Sandy, arriving by taxi outside the casino.

"Come on in and have a drink," Jonathan said, "You've got to see this place before we leave for the ship."

The pair tipped the croupier, then cashed out their chips at the banker's window. They saw the girls entering from across the entrance atrium, each holding several shopping bags.

"How did you boys do at the tables?" Sandy inquired, planting a kiss on her husband's cheek.

"Probably not as good as you two did," Tanner laughed, pointing at the shopping bags.

"We had such fun," Carolyn said. "This is such a gorgeous place, don't you love it?"

"We had a good day too," Jonathan said, "but this Casino was the highlight of our day. I broke even and Tanner won $3000."

"That will just about cover what I spent today." Laughed Sandy, holding up one of the shopping bags with 'Gucci' emblazoned on it.

"Yikes, I was afraid of that," Tanner said.

"You high rollers promised us a drink, didn't you?" Carolyn asked.

"Yes, we sure did," Jonathan said. "The bar is over there."

Entering the ornate lounge, a distinguished man escorted the group to a linen covered table. He then helped the girls with their packages and seated the group.

"Mesdames et Messieurs, may I take your order for something refreshing to drink?" the waiter asked.

"My wife will have a Long Island Iced Tea, and I'll have a Vesper Martini," Tanner replied.

"A glass of Merlot for me, and a light beer for my wife, please, Jonathan added.

"Very good, thank you. I will be back shortly with your drinks," the waiter said. "Would you like an aperitif perhaps?" he added.

"No thank you, we'll be heading back to our ship soon." Tanner replied.

"Very well," the waiter said, bowing slightly as he exited.

"Have you noticed how friendly everyone has been?" Sandy asked. "The people are so gracious."

"Maybe it's because we're spending money like some crazy American lottery winners," remarked Tanner."

"That's a possibility," Jonathan added.

"I'm just sayin'," Tanner said, laughing.

"I would just like to think that the people of Monaco are all naturally very warm and welcoming people." Sandy said.

"My dear Sandy," Tanner replied, "money from rich tourists is what brings out the best manners in our European friends, I'm afraid to say."

"Don't you think that's being a tad pessimistic, Tanner?" Carolyn asked.

"People are not always motivated by money. Some are genuinely happy to have strangers visit their country – don't you think Carolyn?" Sandy asked, shifting her response.

Carolyn agreed. "We've met several people on this trip who had nothing to gain financially by being helpful and friendly."

Tanner knew he was out-voted on this one. He looked at Jonathan, who by now was smiling broadly, enjoying the debate between Tanner and the girls.

"I think we may have been a little harsh, Tanner. The girls are right, money is not always the motivator," Jonathan said.

Knowing he had run out of confederates, Tanner quickly changed the conversation.

"Well, I'm anxious to see what awaits us in Barcelona."

The group finished their drinks, and as the waiter placed the bill on the table, Sandy made it a point to tip him 100 Euros.

"Nice waiter," she said, looking straight at Tanner.

***

Barcelona, Spain proved to be one of the group's favorite stops on their itinerary. Rich in history, music and dance, a single day in the city could hardly be considered adequate. But much to their surprise and delight, they discovered the wonderful Spanish tradition of 'Tapas.'

Throughout the city, hundreds of 'Tapas bars' can be found, and to the delight of the couples, they found several of them. 'Tapas' are simply small appetizers served in the local bars, consisting of individual helpings of seafood, deep fried pastries, filled with chicken, beef or vegetables. Each location has its own special assortment of Tapas. One Café featured ham croquettes, deep fried breaded ham, while another offered small pizzas, with ham, sausage or mushrooms. Tanner and Jonathan were in appetizer heaven wherever they went, from small neighborhood bars to local cafes.

Their next stop was the Isle of Mallorca, an island off the coast of Spain. There the couples enjoyed a private chartered cruise on the 'Vita Bel,' a beautiful sailing yacht. It was a perfect day of sailing, punctuated by a couple of stops in secluded bays to enjoy snorkel diving in the pristine waters.

Next, the Noordam sailed on to Tunisia, Sicily and Naples. The 20 - day itinerary then brought them back to Rome, followed by stops in Croatia and Greece, including the amazingly beautiful islands of Corfu and Santorini.

The final leg of the journey would take them to Ephesus, back to Naples, and finally back to Rome.

The foursome spent their last night in Rome at the St. Regis before their flight home the following day. After breakfast, Tanner announced to Sandy there was a special place he wanted her to see before leaving Rome. Tanner made arrangements through the hotel's concierge for a limousine and a driver.

"Where are you taking me Mr. Riley?" Sandy laughed as they stepped into the car. A few seconds later they were weaving their way through the streets of Rome.

"I want to take you out for one last Gelato and one special souvenir." Tanner said.

Soon the limousine came to a stop in front of Tiffany's. Tanner exited the car, while the driver opened Sandy's door. Taking his wife's hand, Tanner led Sandy to one of the beautiful store window displays for which Tiffany's is famous. Speaking softly in a tone that reminded Sandy of their engagement day, Tanner revealed his plan.

"Sandy, since this is the last day of our amazing European vacation, I wanted to give you something special. Something that will bring back these wonderful memories each time you wear it."

Tanner pointed out a beautiful diamond encrusted oval cocktail watch, prominently displayed in the window.

"Remember the watch that you admired?"

"It's gorgeous." Sandy whispered.

As she looked up at Tanner's smiling face, she could feel her eyes brimming with tears.

"I knew you liked it," Tanner said, "so I didn't think you would mind if I bought it for you."

The tears now rolled down Sandy's cheeks as she rummaged through her purse to find a tissue.

"Come on, let's try it on." Tanner said, grabbing Sandy's hand and guiding her through the gilded glass doors.

There, Tiffany's manager, a sophisticated fiftyish woman, retrieved the $22,000, diamond – trimmed watch from behind the counter. She opened the ornate box and slipped it on Sandy's slender wrist.

"How very lovely," she said as she fastened the clasp on the black silk wrist band.

"Yes, very lovely," Tanner repeated, focusing his attention on Sandy's smiling face.

"And the watch is pretty too."

Chapter 13

Tecate Tango

Mario Gutierrez arrived in San Diego by bus, carrying only a small backpack. His well thought out plan was a gamble, yet the only solution he could think of, to someday live life free from the shadow of Carlos Flores. Like the nightmare he experienced some months prior, he was also well aware that this gamble could literally cost him his life.

Now that he was near the border, he needed to make his way into Mexico without being detected. This part he was confident about, for he had crossed both into Mexico and into the United States undetected, over a hundred times. It was his job and he was good at it. His crossings in the past were much more dangerous, considering the risks of crossing while carrying hundreds of thousands of dollars in drug cartel cash or tightly wrapped kilos of cocaine. But those were the days when, in his prime, he had the backing of Carlos Flores. Now, having betrayed Carlos, he operated under what was certainly a death sentence. But he must put all that behind him now and concentrate on finding the tunnel.

Among the bragging rights of drug smugglers, none are more legitimate that those of "Fat Man" Flores and his masterfully dug tunnels. Mario in his earlier days had assisted Flores in choosing locations for some of his tunneling projects, which rivaled those of their competitor, El Chapo Guzman.

The price of securing real estate and the hiring of skillful engineers, can drive the cost of a tunnel to over one million dollars. In some areas near the Otay Mesa border checkpoint, several of these tunnels were discovered by border patrol investigators and followed in both directions to their source. In some cases, a tunnel would start from a warehouse in an industrial area and end at a private home in Mexico. Both properties were strategically located and purchased by the cartel. These installations were very effective and many are in full operation to this day, allowing smugglers to transport tons of drugs north and millions of dollars south.

Flores, although not a pioneer of tunneling, was certainly an innovator when it came to streamlining the tunnel building process. For over ten years, "Fat Man" Flores maintained an exclusive business relationship with a mining engineer and a team of experienced "drillers" from the mining region of Durango. These engineers, equipped with air compressors, jackhammers, and portable rail-mounted ore carts, were capable of moving enormous amounts of earth under the cover of darkness. Their projects were legendary, and Flores paid his drillers handsomely. So well designed were the Fat Man's tunnels, very few of them were ever discovered by authorities. It was to one of these that Mario was now headed.

Soon after arriving at the bus terminal in San Diego, Mario boarded the line 894 bus, which would take him to Tecate, California, a 40 - mile, 2 - hour jaunt through rural hill country. This small unincorporated town sits adjacent to its Mexican counterpart - Tecate, Mexico. Many Mexicans as well as Americans use this small border town crossing as an alternative to the San Ysidro crossing south of San Diego. Mario, though, was here to cross the border in his own fashion – underground and undetected, through the 'Tecate Tunnel,' a closely guarded, drug runner's secret. To do this successfully, the young man waited for darkness to fall.

In a town of 200 people, Mario knew that he may stand out as suspicious if he lingered too long in the small village. He had, by plan, managed to arrive near dusk and make his way to a small restaurant near the border crossing facility. By now, hungry and thirsty from his day-long journey, the young man ordered a cheese enchilada and a cold Tecate beer. Taking his time, Mario finished his meal and ordered another beer. It was dark by the time he paid his check - time to make his way to the tunnel.

Years ago, Mario arranged for the purchase of a small auto body shop on the American side of Tecate. Its owner, the brother of one of Carlos Flores' most trusted men, agreed to continue to run the shop as usual. Carlos brought in his engineers to start tunneling each evening until the early hours of the morning. The location was perfect, with no homes or foot traffic nearby. As long as the former owner cooperated with the cartel, he would operate the body shop and prosper. In addition, Carlos paid the operator a hefty $500 in cash for every large transit through the tunnel, keeping him happy, quiet and content.

At the same time, on the Mexican side of Tecate, Mario and Carlos arranged for a second transaction. Exactly 1,000 feet from the body shop was a machine shop, perfectly located in an industrial area similar to the body shop – with little to no traffic after business hours. The owner of the machine shop was facing hard economic times. His business had operated for 20 years in that location, but business had slowed to a crawl. When Mario got the word that the business was for sale he immediately purchased the property at full price. A new 'cartel-friendly' manager ran the business in its normal fashion, while providing the 'engineers' access to the property to construct the second half of the tunnel. It was a perfect combination for "Fat Man" Flores and the cartel. Within a year the tunnel was competed - and since then, untold billions of dollars in drugs and cash have transited the 'Tecate Tunnel.'

Twenty minutes after leaving the restaurant, Mario arrived at the body shop. In the darkness, the young man instinctively moved to the rear of the building and located the built-in roof access ladder. He climbed effortlessly up the metal rungs to the rooftop. Looking around from his rooftop perch, he saw no one, and with the exception of a few barking dogs in a distant neighborhood, heard nothing of concern. Walking across the flat roof, he came to the roof access hatch, which, as expected, was locked with a padlock. Mario removed the backpack from his shoulders and laid it on the rooftop. Locating a small flashlight from inside the backpack, he found a set

109

of lock picks, arranged on a key ring. Within a minute the young man had picked the lock and opened the roof access hatch. He peered down through the opening to see nothing but darkness. Clenching his flashlight in his teeth, he climbed down the metal ladder into the shop, carefully closing the hatch behind him. He moved to the southwest corner of the building where the tunnel opening was concealed under a large rubber floor mat. It opened easily, just as Mario remembered. After shutting the hatch behind him, he climbed vertically down the 15 steps leading to the horizontal shaft of the tunnel. In less than twenty minutes Mario had traversed the dank and dusty 1,000 feet of the 'Tecate Tunnel' and reached the vertical exit shaft on the Mexican side. Climbing up the ladder, the young man gently pushed up on the overhead hatch revealing a pitch dark workshop with not a soul in sight. Pushing the hatch all the way open, Mario climbed the remaining rungs of the ladder and stepped out into the room. He shut the hatch quietly behind him, making sure there was no sign of disturbance. From the hatchway, Mario moved to the rear entrance of the building. After examining the area with his flashlight, he determined the building was not alarmed, making it safe to exit quietly out the back door.

Stepping into the night air, Mario looked around and sniffed a familiar smell. "Ah… Mexico!" he whispered quietly to himself. It had been over a year since setting foot in his homeland and for a brief moment it felt very good, but instinctively his thoughts returned soberly to his plan of action. This was no time for complacency or celebration. He must keep his vigilance keen, he reminded himself, for his plan to be successful.

The young man headed a few blocks toward the town center, mingling with the crowds who were enjoying their balmy Saturday night strolls around Parque Hidalgo. Mario was captured by the sight of happy families, the music of the mariachis, and the smell of the street food. He longed for the day that he could be part of a scene like this, and not merely an out of place observer.

Mario walked into the Hotel Tecate, where for $21 he rented a room for the night. It was clean and basic, everything he needed for a good night's sleep.

***

The driver carefully parked the limousine parallel to the garage door of Tanner and Sandy's condominium.

"This is perfect," Tanner said, opening the passenger door and exiting. Assisting the driver, they unloaded the luggage, from the rear of the Lincoln, into the garage. After tipping the driver, he thanked them and drove off - leaving Tanner and Sandy standing alone in the driveway.

"Home sweet home," Sandy said, smiling.

"It's good to be back," Tanner said, as he hoisted two of their bags through the garage towards the back door. Stopping at the door, he put down the luggage and punched a few keys on his security alarm control box.

"That's strange," Tanner said.

"What's strange?" asked Sandy.

"When I first opened the garage door, there was no alarm alert, and now the whole thing seems to be dead."

"I'll call the alarm company tomorrow," Sandy said, matter-of-factly, "I'll add it to my long list of things to do."

After stowing their luggage in a walk-in closet, the couple made a quick tour of the house, checking everything from room to room.

"Well, everything looks the same as we left it." Tanner observed.

"It's so nice to be home," Sandy said, "but you know what I'm going to miss?"

"What's that?" Tanner asked.

"Every evening our room steward left a chocolate mint on our pillows for us. It was a small thing, but it made me feel special."

"You are special," Tanner said, pulling Sandy towards him. "And if you wish, I'll leave a mint on your pillow for the rest of your life."

"Tanner Riley, you are so sweet."

The couple spent the evening recapturing favorite moments of their vacation. Each port and city had been special, in its own way. They poured through hundreds of photos taken and by the end of the evening they concluded that this had been the best month of their lives.

"I guess that now is the time to get back to the routine of normal people, leading normal lives." Sandy observed.

"I'm actually looking forward to that," Tanner said. "But when you think about it, our circumstances are far from normal. This vacation doesn't have to be a 'once in a lifetime' event. We have the luxury of enjoying this whenever we like."

"And I have you to thank for that Tanner Riley." Sandy said, embracing her husband.

Tanner kissed her on the forehead.

"I feel like the richest man on earth - and it has nothing to do with the lottery - but because I have you."

***

Mario checked out of the Hotel Tecate early, and then headed two blocks down Juarez Avenue to the bus terminal. The next stop on the young man's itinerary was Tijuana, where, unannounced, he hoped to have a private meeting with Carlos Flores. Mario knew Flores to be a somewhat reasonable man, so he was confident that he would at least be heard by him. How the "Fat Man" would respond to the young man's story would be anyone's guess. Mario purchased his $4 ticket for the 2 ½ hour trip, and then boarded the bus, which was scheduled to leave within minutes.

The road to Tijuana was a winding one, through hilly countryside and steep canyons. This was an area that Mario was very familiar with, for along this route were several trails used by human mules to transport drugs into the United States. In years past, he had used some of these trails himself, but the tunnels changed much of that. Marijuana, Cocaine and Methamphetamines were now simply moved through tunnels into the U.S. and loaded into vehicles. Once loaded, the skilled driver would choose the best route to his destination - usually Los Angeles, San Francisco, or Las Vegas. Some large shipments were hidden in vehicles, which were driven onto car hauler trailers, then trucked to their destination. Experienced drivers were paid handsomely to deliver their cargo on-time, while avoiding the dreaded border checkpoints and the most dangerous threat of all – drug sniffing dogs.

The squealing brakes of the bus awoke Mario from his brief nap. Looking out the dusty window the young man at once recognized his surroundings. The bus was arriving at Terminal de Autobuses, a few blocks from the border crossing in downtown Tijuana - the end of the line. Stepping off of the bus, the young man walked into the terminal building. After finding the restroom, he returned to the lunch counter and ordered a torta and a Coke.

Outside the terminal building a long line of taxis could be seen at the curbside, their drivers patiently waiting for travelers arriving at the terminal. The young man approached the closest cab, a bright yellow VW, and caught the attention of the driver.

"Where would you like to go, Senor?" the cabbie asked.

"Up there." Mario replied, pointing to the top of the hill, overlooking the city. He handed the cabbie a post-it note with the address on it. "Do you know how to find this address?" He asked.

"Si, this is a very nice area - Zona Diamonte."

"I need you to take me there," Mario said.

He could sense that the driver was burning with curiosity about his new passenger. The address to which they were heading was the most prestigious area in all of Tijuana. Large homes, perched upon the hillsides, with commanding views of the city, including Agua Caliente and the Tijuana Country Club below. Looking around the neighborhood, encapsulated among the squalor of the surrounding areas, it would be difficult to discern that one was in Mexico, much less Tijuana.

"Do you live here my friend?" the cabbie asked, as he artfully maneuvered the Volkswagen up the steep and winding streets.

"No." Mario replied.

"Very rich people live up here!"

"That's what they say," Mario replied under his breath.

A few minutes later the driver located the address and came to a stop in front of a fashionable two story house with a large gated entrance. Behind the partially opened iron gates, a black Chevy Suburban with dark tinted windows and a white BMW were parked.

"This is good." Mario said, collecting his belongings and paying the driver.

"Could you wait one minute while I make sure my friend is home?

"Sure, no problem," The cabbie replied. "just give me a 'thumbs up.'"

Mario took a deep breath, arched his shoulders, twisted his head sharply to the left, cracking his neck, then walked through the gate and up the steps of Carlos Flores' home. He rang the doorbell. After what seemed an eternity, the door opened and Mario could see only a faint outline of a person through the security screen.

"Hello?" It was a young woman's voice – timid, young and sweet.

"Mario?" The voice was less timid – now sounding vaguely familiar.

"Mario Gutierrez?" The security screen opened – it was Carlos' daughter, Isadora.

"Isadora, is that you?" Mario exclaimed.

"Yes, it's me! What are you doing here?" The teenager embraced the young man.

"I've come to see your father. Is he here?"

"Yes, he's here, but Mario, he has nothing good to say about you. I'm afraid he might hurt you. You should go!" The young woman was now visibly emotional.

Mario turned to the taxi driver and gave him a thumbs-up gesture. The cabbie responded with a wave, and then drove away.

"I've come a long way and I need to talk to him," Mario said, with his tone even and insistent.

Just then, Carlos appeared at the door, followed by two of his security men.

"Izzy, come in and go to your room please." Carlos' tone with his daughter was firm but not angry. He waited until his daughter was out of earshot before turning his attention to Mario.

"Hello Mario, you look healthy, although a bit thin, I must say." Carlos said.

"Hello Carlos. I'm glad to see you. I've come a long way and I have many things I must say to you." Mario's voice was contrite but nervous.

"I received your letter and the key," Carlos said, calmly.

"Did you find the money?" the young man asked.

"Yes. We sent Luis to find and return the money at great risk to us. It was all there, every dollar."

"I'm sorry Carlos to have put you at risk. I should have brought the money back myself," Mario said.

"You should not have taken it in the first place!" Carlos snapped. Carlos looked at his men and then at Mario.

"Let's go into my office." Carlos motioned with his head.

The four men walked through the huge vaulted living room, then down a long hallway to Carlos' office. Carlos sat down behind his desk and motioned Mario to have a seat. The two security men stood back on each side of Mario, out of his field of vision.

"I'm truly sorry Carlos." Mario's voice was nearly a whisper. "I have struggled for over a year, trying to figure out how to make this right. I…I cannot change what I have done, but I swear to you I will never be disloyal to you again."

Carlos lit a cigarette then leaned back in his chair.

"You know… it was not just the money," Carlos said, tilting his head upwards and blowing a plume of smoke into the air.

"I gave you great responsibilities, because after many years I came to trust you like my own brother."

The young man looked down.

"I have been living with this shame and fear for a long time. Hiding like an animal," Mario confessed.

"Hiding?" Carlos asked, his eyes opening wide. "You mean in your little rooming house in Huntington Beach? At the Home Depot? Or at your job at the little market? Did you really think you were hiding?"

Mario looked up, trying to grasp what Flores just said.

"I could have had you killed any time within the last eight months, my friend. You should have known that. You cannot hide from me."

"Then why have you let me live?" Mario could now feel tears welling up in his eyes. He was determined not to blink, not to let Carlos see the tears run down his face.

"I let you live because I hoped that you would come to your senses and someday return – as you have today."

Mario blinked.

"I don't know what to say." The tears were now unstoppable, overflowing and running down both cheeks.

Carlos stood and dismissed his men, then turned back to the young man. Holding out his hand to the young man, Carlos said in a kind voice, "I'm glad to see you Mario. Welcome home."

"Thank you Carlos" Mario said, standing to shake Carlos' giant hand. After shaking hands the men embraced. Carlos patted the young man on the back firmly.

"There are no words to describe the relief you have just given me."

"Does that mean you will come back to work for me?" Carlos asked.

"Actually I have something I need to tell you that you will find very interesting." Mario said.

Carlos snuffed out his cigarette in an ashtray and again, motioned for the young man to sit down.

"I'm listening." Carlos said as he resumed his seated position behind his desk.

"A few months ago I got a job at a small market near my little apartment…." Mario began.

"Trung's Neighborhood Market," Carlos interjected.

"Yes, that's correct," the young man said. "One of my duties was selling lottery tickets to Mr. Trung's customers. One day a man I had never met before came into the store and asked to buy 10,000 lottery tickets. I asked him if he often purchased so many tickets and he told me a lie. He said that it was his rich boss who often bought thousands of lottery tickets."

Carlos interrupted. "How do you know he lied to you?"

"Because," Mario continued, "a few weeks later I saw the same man on the TV news – he and his friend had just won $85 million in the California lottery!"

Carlos shifted forward in his chair, his arms resting on the desktop.

"$85 million?

Mario continued. "Yes, one of the largest jackpots ever won in California. But, one of the men who won told the interviewer that he had simply chosen a few of his favorite numbers – and one of them just happened to be the lucky one. So I did some checking on the two men and discovered that one of the men works as an insurance company actuary – a job that requires a high degree of mathematic skills. I then learned that the two men and their wives would be out of the country on a cruise for several weeks. While they were gone, I broke into the mathematician's house to see if I could find out more about his lottery win."

"And?" Carlos asked, sitting on the edge of his swivel chair.

"What I found inside his home and garage, convinced me that these two men have discovered a method to beat the California lottery."

Mario reached inside his backpack and produced a notebook with several pages of photographs.

"Bring your chair around here and let's look at what you have." Carlos said excitedly.

"First of all, there are these." The young man said, placing on Carlos' desk a wad of one hundred lottery tickets bundled together with rubber bands.

"These are just a few of the tickets I found inside two large cardboard boxes in the man's garage."

"How many tickets do you think were inside the boxes?" Carlos asked.

"I took this picture." Mario said, opening up the folder to the first photograph of the two large boxes.

Carlos examined the picture closely. "There must be many, thousands of lottery tickets inside these boxes!" Carlos exclaimed.

"Yes, and they all appear to have the same game date."

"What else do you have there?" By now, Carlos' excitement was palpable.

"Inside the house, in his office, I found this…" Mario turned to a photograph of three printers, arranged in a row.

"Inside the paper tray of this printer I found these…" The next photo was a close-up of the printer tray with blank lottery play slips inside.

"This is how he filled out so many of his lottery cards," Carlos said.

"Yes," agreed Mario, "and as you can see, there were three of these printers and three computers."

Carlos stood and started pacing back and forth behind his desk with his arms folded, his hand to his chin.

"And finally, I found this in his wall safe."

Carlos bent down, placing his hands on his desk to examine Mario's series of photographs which showed the Goldman Sachs financial plan prepared for Tanner and Sandra Riley. Carlos opened his desk drawer and retrieved a magnifying glass to examine the documents more closely.

"This shows that our mathematician split the proceeds with his brother-in-law Jonathan Taylor." Carlos observed. "Their total winnings were nearly $17 million each."

"Yes, Carlos, $17 million each. But it was Tanner Riley who was the brains of the operation. I think his brother-in-law must have been the main investor."

"Can you imagine having this man's ability to win lotteries?" Carlos said. "Nearly every country in the world has its own lottery. The possibilities would be endless!"

"At first it seemed impossible that anyone could do this," Mario said, "but the evidence is undeniable."

"Have you told anyone else about this man?"

Mario shook his head.

"No. You and I are the only ones who know about this."

"For now, that is," Carlos said, "and if we don't move on this soon, someone else will."

He knew that other criminal organizations would stop at nothing to have this man win tens of millions of dollars in cash with very little risk. But how to convince Tanner Riley to cooperate was the question.

Carlos lit another cigarette and sat down in his chair.

"We first need to discover how he does this. What is his formula? We need to determine if this is something that can be duplicated by our organization.

"Do you have a plan in mind?" Mario asked.

"Let me think about this," Carlos replied. "I have someone in mind that can help us with this. And I can assure you Mario; you will be paid handsomely for bringing this man to our attention."

"I am very happy to do this, Carlos. It's the least I can do to make amends for the trouble I caused you."

"Now, you will stay here at my home tonight – agreed?"

"Yes sir, thank you." Mario responded.

"How did you get here?"

Mario described his trip by bus to San Diego, then to Tecate, through the tunnel and on to Tijuana.

"You used the tunnel?" asked Carlos, incredulously.

"Yes sir. It was no problem at all."

"You should have called. I would have sent a car!" Carlos burst out laughing. "You traveled all the way to the Tecate tunnel to enter Mexico!"

Mario joined Carlos in laughter that lasted several seconds, until they almost cried. It felt good to laugh, Mario thought. He had not laughed in over a year.

Chapter 14

911 Heaven

The Riley's parked their car and walked across the lot into the new car showroom on Pacific Coast highway. It was a beautiful Saturday morning, with a cloudless sky. Tanner had cajoled Sandy into accompanying him to this Newport Beach Porsche dealership to fulfill one of his life-long dreams – buying a new Porsche 911.

Unlike past car buying experiences, the couple was not besieged by a car salesman before they got through the door. It appeared this would be a much more sophisticated experience. Approaching the main desk Tanner spoke to the receptionist.

"Hello, I'm looking for Robert."

"Robert Espinoza?" she asked, reaching for the phone.

"Yes, we have an appointment."

In a few seconds, Robert answered his page from the receptionist.

"Robert, a gentleman is here to see you – a Mister…" she paused and looked at the young couple.

"Riley, Tanner Riley"

"Mr. Tanner Riley," the receptionist repeated.

"He will be right here," she said, smiling as she hung up the phone.

Tanner's attention shifted to a gleaming white Turbo 911 Cabriolet on the showroom floor.

"Nice," Tanner said admiringly, walking to the car - lightly caressing the smooth lines of the driver's door. Sandy joined him and began carefully examining the window sticker.

"Only $208,000, Tanner."

"And probably worth every dime of it," Tanner replied.

Just then the sales associate, Robert, appeared.

"Tanner, right? And this must be Sandy."

Robert shook hands with them and introduced himself.

"I'm Robert Espinoza, the one you spoke with on the phone the other day about your interest in purchasing a Porsche."

"My husband has dreamed of owning a Porsche for as long as I've known him, but it's always been that $208,000 thing that's prevented him from getting it," Sandy said, pointing her thumb over her shoulder toward the window sticker.

"I completely understand," Robert responded. "These automobiles do command a high price, but I can honestly say that because of their quality, their history and their unmatched performance, they are worth the price."

"Well I'm happy to say that not only do I agree with you Robert, but I've finally come to terms with the price tag," Tanner interjected. "In fact, if we find the right car at the right price, I plan on writing a check for the full price and then driving out of here in a new Porsche."

"So where do we start?" Sandy asked.

"How about right here," Robert suggested. "What do you think about this convertible, Sandy?"

Sandy opened the driver's door and settled into the black leather seat. "I love this car," she said, stroking the upholstery with her hand. "These seats are so comfortable."

"As much as I like this Cabriolet, I think I'd prefer a coupe," Tanner said.

"OK, that sounds like something we can take care of," Robert said. "Let's go out here and let me show you a new 911 Turbo S that just came in."

The trio exited the showroom and walked a short distance to a shaded parking area where a metallic silver Turbo coupe was parked.

"Wow!" exclaimed Tanner. "Now, this is what I'm talking about!"

Robert opened the driver's door.

"Get in and see how it feels."

Climbing in, Tanner soon had the seat adjusted to his liking and invited Sandy to join him.

"What does the 'S' stand for?" asked Sandy.

"It means sport," replied Robert. "This car literally could be taken to the track and raced. The 3.8 litre engine is a twin turbo, 6 cylinder, that produces 560 horsepower. Would you like to take a test drive?"

"I would love to drive this car," Tanner said excitedly.

With Robert in the rear jump seat, and Sandy in the passenger's seat, Tanner maneuvered the 911 out of the lot and south on Coast Highway.

"If you have the time," Robert said, "I'd suggest we head down to Laguna to the 133 and buzz down Laguna Canyon Road."

"Oh, we've got plenty of time," Sandy laughed.

"Did you notice how smooth the acceleration is Tanner?" Robert asked.

"Sweet," Tanner replied.

"This car is equipped with an all-wheel-drive, seven speed transmission with rear axle steering. It can detect if you over steer, under steer, or do anything else to lose stability. The Stability

Management System automatically applies braking on individual wheels to restore stability. Pretty cool, huh?"

"Very cool."

Tanner wound through the Coast Highway traffic and turned East on Laguna Canyon Road. Although the traffic was to be expected on a Saturday, he found it a pleasure negotiating the gentle winding canyon road. Sandy discovered the controls for the sunroof and slid it all the way back - enjoying the wind in her hair.

As they approached Interstate 5, Robert suggested another challenging route.

"If you want a real nice road course, we can go on down the 5 to Ortega Highway," Robert suggested.

"I love that road," Tanner said, "let's do it!"

Punching it, Tanner eased the Porsche onto the freeway and eased off the throttle when the speedometer read 90 miles per hour.

"Jeez, this car is quick!" Tanner exclaimed.

"Keep in mind you're pushing 560 horsepower," Robert said, "her top speed is 200, so be careful."

A few minutes later they arrived at the Ortega Highway exit, where Tanner guided the car through the twists and turns of the scenic, rural canyon road. As they reached the lookout point overlooking Lake Elsinore, Tanner pulled over at the rest stop where the trio got out and stretched their legs.

"What do you think about this amazing car, Sandy?" Tanner asked.

"I really like it. I think you should buy it," Sandy replied. "We have the money – you worked hard to earn it – I think we should just do it."

Tanner pulled Sandy close to him and kissed her on her forehead. "Thank you, Sandy. You are an amazing woman."

"And you, Tanner Riley, are an amazing guy yourself – plus you drive a pretty bitchin' car," she said with a wink.

The couple walked back to the car where Robert was waiting, admiring the view of Lake Elsinore below.

"We want the car, Robert," Tanner said, matter-of-factly.

"Uh…great!" Robert replied – trying to mask his surprise.

"There are a couple of things I wanted to tell you about this particular car. It has just about every updated option you can find in a 911, such as Automatic Slip Control, Automatic Brake Differential, PTV Plus, and multi-link rear suspension."

"What does that all mean, Robert?" Sandy asked inquisitively.

"It means this is a bitchin' 911," Tanner laughed.

Robert addressed Sandy's question, describing the research and development that Porsche had invested for decades in their high performance race cars. He explained that these technological improvements have been integrated into Porsche automobiles, making them faster, safer and better handling.

"We'll take it!" Sandy said.

"But besides the amazing handling of this Porsche," Robert continued, "you have creature comforts, like Bluetooth audio, Sirius XM radio, LED headlights with Porsche dynamic lighting system, Homelink garage door opener and a 7 - inch color touch screen, Bose high-end Surround Sound with 12 speakers, seat heaters, luggage net, Porsche entry & drive ignition system, electric glass sunroof, power steering, telephone module, leather interior, sports clock, 20" Sport Classic wheels, illuminated door-sill guards in stainless steel, clear glass taillights, painted center console trim and the classic ornamental Porsche hood crest."

"Robert, we'll take the car!" Tanner reiterated.

"Awesome!" Robert exclaimed, with a fist pump. "You won't be sorry, I promise."

"I tend to agree with you Robert," Tanner said. "I guess we should get back to Newport and wrap this up."

Two and a half hours and $213,000 later, Tanner Riley drove out of the dealership, with the car that most men can only dream of. Sandy followed in Tanner's Honda. Halfway home, Tanner's phone rang. It was Sandy.

"Hey, I just wondered where are we going to put your Honda if you park the Porsche in the garage?"

"I guess I'll put an ad for it on Craigslist."

"I have a better idea." Sandy said.

"What's that?"

"I know a sweet couple with a very sick child at CHOC whose old car just blew it's transmission. I was thinking your Honda might make their life a little easier right now."

"That's what I love about you Sandy."

"I know you do baby. I know you do."

Chapter 15

Bring In Tony

'Fat Man' Flores was just finishing his breakfast – a special treat that his wife, Esmeralda, prepared for him each Sunday morning. When the phone rang, Carlos picked it up quickly, hoping it was the call he had been expecting.

"Hello."

Carlos was right, the caller was Tony Telemontes.

"Antonio, it's good to hear you, my friend," Carlos said.

Antonio Telmontes was Carlos most trusted friend and business partner. For the last two years he served as liaison between the Tijuana organization and their people in Columbia. Telemontes was instrumental in branching out the cartel, in an effort to decentralize their operation.

"I came as soon as I could, Carlos. Your message sounded urgent."

"Thank you Antonio. Are you at the airport? I'll send a car to pick you up."

"That won't be necessary, I'm driving there now. I should be there within a half hour."

"Excellent. We have much to talk about," replied Carlos.

Upon arriving, Carlos greeted his old friend with a firm handshake and a bear hug.

"It's good to see you again Carlos!" Antonio exclaimed. "You are looking good. Esmeralda must be taking good care of you."

Just then, Esmeralda and her daughter Isadora appeared.

"Antonio, it has been so long since we have seen you," Esmeralda said as she embraced the older man.

Antonio then caught sight of Isadora.

"Oh My God!" Telemontes shouted. "Tell me this is not Isadora!"

"Hola tio Tony."

Antony embraced the teenage girl, then stood back to look at her.

"I am amazed at how you have grown since I last saw you. You are so beautiful, Meja."

"She is only sixteen and already I have to chase the boys away." Carlos said.

The reunion moved into the kitchen, where Esmeralda served coffee and snacks, prepared for their special guest.

"We were hoping that you could stay for dinner Antonio," Esmeralda said.

At that moment, Mario entered the room.

"Ah, Mario, I want you to meet a good friend of mine, Antonio Telemontes. You may have heard of him," Carlos said.

"Yes, Antonio, I am honored to finally meet you," the young man said, shaking Telemonte's hand.

Telemontes, although 60 years old, with silver gray hair was slim and athletic. His reputation among cartel members was legendary. For many years it had been rumored that Antonio was good friends with Fidel Castro, partially explaining his never-ending source of expensive Cuban cigars. But his influence was not limited to Cuba. Telemontes was known far and wide throughout Central and South America, as well as Mexico and the Caribbean.

Carlos invited both men to his office, motioning for them to sit down in two large stuffed leather chairs. Pulling up his rolling chair from behind his desk, He explained to both men at the outset that their discussion was to remain confidential. No other members of the organization were to be informed until a final plan was clearly agreed upon. Carlos was taking no chances of being embarrassed with a plan that was not well thought out and perfect in every detail.

"I've asked you to be here, Antonio, because I value your judgment and experience. Your advice in the past has been very helpful to me - and this situation, I feel, demands the scrutiny of a man like yourself. So, I'm first going to ask Mario to lay out some very interesting details for us about two American gentlemen named Jonathan Taylor and Tanner Riley."

The young man began by recounting his chance meeting with a man named Jonathan, who requested to buy 10,000 lottery tickets. Mario explained how he personally processed these tickets for the man, who claimed to have purchased them for his wealthy boss. Later, however, he saw this same man and his partner, Tanner Riley, on the television news. Tanner Riley, a mathematician lied when asked by a newsman how he had chosen his winning lottery number.

Mario showed the details of his investigation into these two men, including the break-in of the Riley's condominium in Huntington Beach.

Opening his folder of photographs, he explained step by step his search of the residence and the evidence he discovered. Telemontes, studied the photos of the boxes of lottery tickets, the printers and the financial prospectus showing the investment plan for the 85 million dollar lottery win.

"What do you think, Antonio? Carlos asked.

Antonio leaned back in the leather chair and blew a plume of Cuban cigar smoke into the air.

"Mario – I am impressed. It is plain to see you have done an excellent job of investigating this man. My question to you is this; what is your gut feeling about this man's ability to pick winning lottery numbers?"

"From the moment I saw this man buy thousands of dollars of tickets, I, of course, became very curious. I could not get it out of my head that possibly Mr. Riley has discovered some formula – some method to win the lottery. I knew that the only way I could determine the truth of the matter would be to examine his home," Mario said, holding up the notebook of photographs. "This proves to me, beyond a doubt, this man has discovered a method to beat the lottery."

Telemontes looked into the young man's eyes and saw his expression of rock-solid conviction. He then looked at Carlos.

"What are your thoughts Carlos? Is this Tanner Riley for real?"

Carlos response was equally certain.

"Yes, Antonio. I think the evidence speaks for itself. He is for real."

Antonio looked at both men, then walked over to Mario and took the photographs from the young man. Flipping from page to page as he paced across the room, he then turned to the men again.

"I must admit that I too am convinced that we may have a very useful asset here. Imagine the possibilities if we could harness this ability. But there are important questions that we must find the answers to."

Carlos was the first to respond.

"My question is, how do we make this work for us? Do we take this formula from him and use it for ourselves? Do we convince him, or must we force him to work for us?"

"My main concern is, can Tanner Riley repeat his lottery win?" Mario added.

"Yes, I agree," Antonio said. "We need to know how his system works, and how consistent it is. There is always the possibility this big win of his was a 'flash in the pan,' as they say."

"So it boils down to this," Carlos said. "For us to determine what the formula is and how it works; there is only one effective way that I know."

Everyone in the room knew the answer, but it was 'Fat Man' Flores, who was the first to verbalize it.

"We need to bring this man and his wife down to Tecate and have a little talk with him."

Flores' voice had suddenly taken on a cruel tone. "I guarantee he will answer all of our questions about his formulas."

"But wouldn't it be risky, - kidnapping an American couple and bringing them to Mexico for interrogation?" Mario asked.

Antonio was quick to answer.

"Mario, let me tell you something about risk. You, of all people should be very familiar with the risks that we take in this business. Every mule we send into the states, every airplane loaded with cocaine, carries risk. Our tunnels – dug at risk by our engineers at the cost of hundreds of thousands of dollars are constantly at risk of discovery. Yet we justify that risk by examining very carefully the rewards."

Antonio stopped pacing long enough to spark up another cigar. Puffing a few times, until the Cohiba was fully lit, he continued.

"Ah yes, the rewards," he said, holding up the cigar admiringly. "One should always examine the ratio of risk to reward. Let me ask you Mario, what is the potential reward if our lottery boy – Tanner, cooperates with us just one time?"

"He won $86 million just a few months ago," answered Mario.

"$86 million," Antonio repeated.

"How much risk do we run in growing, processing, packaging, transporting and selling $86 million worth of cocaine would you guess Carlos?"

Carlos nodded in agreement.

"There is high risk at every stage of the process – from the production to the sale."

"And then," continued Antonio, "we must transport the cash back into Mexico at even greater risk. Why? Because 1 million dollars worth of cocaine only weighs 44 pounds, while the cash it generates weighs over 250 pounds. But the risk is not over, because now the cash has to be legitimized – laundered to make it appear to have been earned through legal means. Then, and only then, can we enjoy our reward."

Mario realized he had just been schooled by one of the most experienced drug traffickers in the world. His original question now seemed amateurish.

"We need to proceed as soon as possible, before someone else discovers Tanner Riley." Carlos stated.

"I agree," Mario said. Where do we start?"

Chapter 16

The Most Hospitable Kidnapper You Will Ever Meet

The Porsche performed flawlessly as Tanner maneuvered it north through light traffic on Pacific Coast Highway. It was a beautiful sunny day. Just right, thought Tanner, for a drive in his dream car, with his dream girl.

He and Sandy spent the first half of the day in Laguna Beach. After enjoying a breakfast with an ocean view, the couple visited a couple of art galleries and several colorful gift and curio shops along bustling Coast Highway.

Tanner had been anxious to get back on the road. The 911 was little more than a week old and he had yet to put on 100 miles.

Turning into the alleyway leading to his garage, Tanner noticed a large black Suburban turning in behind them. Pressing the remote for the garage door, he carefully pulled the car into the narrow parking space of the garage. The Suburban came to a stop in front of the open garage. Mario Gutierrez emerged from the driver's seat and walked briskly toward the couple. He had a smile on his face, and asked the couple for directions.

"Hey guys, I'm lost, do you know where this address is?"

Pulling a small scrap of paper from his shirt pocket, he showed the couple a scribbled address. Tanner took the paper from the young man, and together with Sandy, they examined the address.

"411 Olive Street," Sandy said, "that's right up the street. You're almost there. Just go out of the alley, turn left and you'll run into Olive."

As Sandy was giving directions, another man exited from the Suburban and walked swiftly toward the couple, drawing a pistol from his waistband. It was Luis Figeroa, a long-time soldier in the Felix cartel.

Pushing the couple into the garage, they pushed the door switch and the garage door closed abruptly behind the group of four. Luis pressed the pistol muzzle firmly into Tanner's ribs.

Sandy's horrified scream lasted only for a second. Mario quickly put one hand over her mouth and grabbed the back of her neck with the other hand.

"Shut up lady!" he said firmly, "We're not here to hurt you, but if you scream one more time I will! Comprende?"

Sandy nodded fearfully before Mario released his grip.

"Please, don't hurt her." Tanner said, his voice trembling.

Mario ordered the couple to move inside the house, and then instructed Luis to park the Suburban in the visitor's parking area. It appeared that no one in the secluded alley had observed the skirmish.

Moving the couple into the house, Mario ordered the couple to sit down on the living room couch. He then called Carlos on his cell phone.

"Hello, we're with them now," Mario said.

"Good," Carlos said, "I'll be standing by. Put me on speaker phone."

"Yes sir," Mario replied, placing the phone on the coffee table in front of the couple.

Soon after, Luis returned from parking their vehicle.

"We're all clear out there," Luis said, pointing behind him with his thumb.

"I'm going to get right to the point with you Mr. and Mrs. Riley," Mario said tersely.

The couple looked at each other, surprised that this man knew their names.

"Yes, I know your names," Mario said, reading the expression on the couple's faces. "And I know much more about you than your names."

"What do you want from us?" Sandy pleaded.

"I have a few questions about your recent lottery win."

"My first question is for you, Mr. Riley. - What became of the two boxes of lottery tickets that were stored in your garage?"

The man's question left Tanner feeling as though he had been punched in the stomach. He immediately knew why these men were here and what they wanted.

"I burned them all in my barbeque."

"Why did you destroy them?" Mario asked.

"Because I didn't want anyone to know that I had purchased them," Tanner admitted.

"How many lottery tickets did you purchase?"

Tanner, realizing that his secret was no longer secure, knew it was futile to hold back anything from these armed men.

"I bought 250,000 tickets."

"Why so many?"

"I think you know why," Tanner said.

"Yes, I know why, but I want to hear it from you. Why exactly 250,000?"

Tanner sighed, looking downward as he answered the man's question.

"It was necessary to buy 250,000 to cover my formula."

"So what you're telling us, is that you have a formula that can pick winning lottery numbers?" Mario asked.

"Yes, - but I've only done it once."

Before Mario had a chance to ask another question, the speaker phone crackled with Carlos voice.

"I have something I would like to say to Mr. and Mrs. Riley," Carlos said.

"Yes sir," Mario replied.

"Mr. Riley, I want you and your wife to know that we have no intentions of harming either of you. But we are going to insist that you cooperate with us fully. Do you understand?"

"Yes, I understand," Tanner said.

"You and your wife are going to be brought to a town in Mexico called Tecate. It is about a four hour trip by car. You will be safe, and you will be treated well, but you must do exactly as I say.

"You're taking us to Mexico?" Sandy exclaimed. "Please… isn't there some other way? Can't we just stay here and tell you everything you need to know?"

"No Mrs. Riley, that is not possible," Carlos answered.

"Mr. Riley, I want you and your wife to bring everything you need with you - Clothes, passports, everything that you may need and will fit into one bag. Is your formula on a computer?" Carlos asked.

"Yes, it's on one of my computers," Tanner answered.

"Good. Bring it and everything you have related to your formula with you. - Do you understand?"

"Yes, I do. But can I please ask if you can take me - and leave Sandy here. I guarantee you that she will not tell a soul... Please!" Tanner begged.

"Mr. Riley, again, I must insist – this is not possible.

"I understand," Tanner said, "We'll cooperate with you. Both of us."

"Excellent," Flores said. "But there is one more detail that we must take care of. - Mario, take me off of the speakerphone."

"Yes sir," Mario said, picking up the phone and placing it to his ear. A short conversation ensued between the two men, ending with Mario saying, "Alright then – we'll see you in a few hours."

"Now we need to take care of an important detail," Mario said. "You will be away for a few days, so I need to know who, among your friends and family, you must contact."

"I'm expected at work on Monday morning," Tanner said.

"I'm off for another day, but I have a shift the day after tomorrow," Sandy added.

"Who else?" Mario asked.

"Well, Jonathan and Carolyn will wonder where we are, Sandy said. "We keep in close touch."

"Anyone else?"

"Not that I can think of," Sandy said.

"I think that just about covers it," Tanner said.

"I want each of you to call your jobs and your relatives. Give them a very convincing reason why you must be gone for a few days. And don't do anything stupid. Do you understand?" Mario said.

"Yes," Tanner said, reaching for his phone.

***

Tanner, Sandy and their captors arrived on the U.S. side of Tecate around 8 p.m. - Tired, frightened and hungry, the couple was blindfolded and then, driven to the body shop that served as the entrance to the 'Tecate Tunnel.' Parking in the rear of the body shop, Mario removed the blindfolds from the couple.

"Are we in Mexico?" Tanner asked, looking out into the blackness of the night.

"We will be soon," Mario replied.

Mario and Luis then ushered the couple, along with all their gear, into the rear entrance of the body shop. Turning on the lights, Luis folded back the tunnel hatch and climbed down the ladder into the tunnel. Mario lowered down a duffel bag containing the couple's belongings along with Tanner's laptop. Then Mario assisted the couple down the ladder and into the tunnel. Luis, carrying a flashlight, led the way through the darkness. Tanner and Sandy followed, with Mario behind the group, lighting their path with his flashlight.

Far ahead, a faint light shining downward could be seen.

"That light is the end of the tunnel," Mario said. "We're in Mexico now."

"So this is one of the tunnels I've read about," Tanner remarked. "Am I to assume that this is a drug cartel tunnel?"

"You are to assume nothing, Mr. Riley," Mario said.

As the group approached the source of the light, it became apparent that the light was shining down into the shaft from an open trap door. Soon the ladder leading up from the shaft came into view. Luis climbed up first, lifting the duffel bag and gear into the room above them.

"Buenas noches, mis hermanos, que finalmente han llegado." The voice from above shouted a welcome to the men climbing up the ladder.

"Is that you Carlos?" Mario shouted, cupping his hands to his mouth.

"Yes – are you hungry?" Carlos asked.

"Yes, we're all hungry and tired," Mario replied.

Sandy ascended the ladder, followed by Tanner and Mario. Climbing up into the lighted room, Tanner looked around to see that he was standing in the middle of a machine shop.

"Welcome to Mexico, Mr. and Mrs. Riley," Carlos said, holding his hand out to shake Tanner's hand, then Sandy's.

"My name is Carlos. This is Antonio, by business partner," Carlos said, placing his hand on Antonio's shoulder. "We are glad that you are here safe and sound. Now you must be very tired and hungry, yes?"

Sandy responded impatiently. "I've got to pee, and I've got to have something to eat!"

Carlos, with a slight smile, barely detectable on his face, looked at Tony, then at Tanner before addressing the angry woman.

"You may use the restroom right over there, Mrs. Riley," Carlos said, pointing to a nearby door. "We will soon have something for you to eat."

Carlos' tone was measured and calm, but it did little to settle Sandy's demeanor.

"Yeah, that's great," Sandy mumbled under her breath as she walked toward the tiny bathroom.

"We've all had a long day, Mrs. Riley," Antonio added.

Whirling around, Sandy replied sharply to the men.

"The difference is, you weren't kidnapped at gunpoint, blindfolded, and driven to God knows where in Mexico!"

Not waiting for a reply, she slammed the restroom door behind her.

The couple was driven from the machine shop to a rural rancho on the outskirts of Tecate. Completely isolated from any other residences, this large home had been a family retreat for Carlos Flores for many years. Typical of the homes in the area, security bars were installed on all windows and doors. The couple was escorted into the house while Luis was sent into town to buy dinner for the hungry group.

Carlos was anxious to get started with questioning Tanner.

"Mr. Riley, while we are waiting for our food to arrive, I would like you to demonstrate to us just how your system works." Carlos said, handing Tanner the laptop computer.

Tired and hungry, Tanner was in no mood to explain this complex program to these men. His mind raced with questions about their fate, now in the hands of armed kidnappers, in a foreign country. His main concern was Sandy, and so complying with his captors, he turned on the computer and placed it on the nearby dining room table. As the screen flickered to life, Antonio, Carlos and Mario huddled around Tanner.

"I'll open up the first part of the program, which is where I enter data into the system."

A data entry screen appeared, with blank boxes appearing in a vertical row.

"This is where I input the numbers that have been drawn for every game, each week."

Scrolling down the page, past the empty boxes, he came to boxes filled in with past lottery numbers.

"You can see here, these empty boxes would have to be filled in with all the past numbers. Once I fill them in, I save them by clicking here."

"That looks simple enough," Mario said. "What happens to all of these saved numbers?"

Tanner opened up another screen on his laptop.

"The new data, together with the past data is now processed with this second program. This is actually the heart of the system, where the data is analyzed and interpreted into a new list of 250,000 sets."

"Is this the list of numbers that you use to purchase the tickets?" Carlos asked.

"Not quite," Tanner said, opening up yet another screen. "I copy the new list and filter it through 3 more processes with this other program."

"What is the purpose of this additional filtering?" Antonio inquired.

"It is a very complex method of re-evaluating the list, deleting some of the choices and adding new combinations," Tanner explained.

"So, can this system be used for any lottery?" Mario asked.

"No," Tanner said. "This system is based only on the California SuperLotto Plus game. All the calculations come from many years of data from this particular game. It would be useless for any other game, because each game has its own unique history and dynamics."

Tanner's demonstration was interrupted 30 minutes later by the arrival of Luis, with containers of hot food for the hungry group. The food was laid out on the dining room table, where everyone helped themselves to beans, rice, tortillas, carne asada, chicken and salsa.

After filling their paper plates, Tanner and Sandy sat together at the end of the large dining room table. "I'm so hungry," Sandy whispered. "And this food looks disgusting."

"Sandy, I'm sorry that you had to be dragged into this," Tanner said, under his breath.

Sandy reached for Tanner's hand. "Let's just give them everything they want and get the hell out of here," she said, looking quickly around the room.

"I don't think it will be that easy," Tanner whispered.

Their captors, although armed and intimidating, showed remarkable restraint with the couple, Tanner thought to himself. Except with the first encounter with their kidnappers, no weapons or violence had since then been displayed. But he knew this could change in an instant. Wondering what their game plan was, Tanner determined that one thing he must never do is give these men everything they asked for. For the couple's own preservation, he was determined that he must remain as the single most important key to these men's success. How he would accomplish this must now be his focus.

After the men finished eating, Carlos sat down at the table with the couple.

"Mr. and Mrs. Riley, we've decided that we will continue our discussion tomorrow morning. It has been a long and stressful day for all of us, so what I think we need now is a good night's sleep. So if you would come with me, I will show you to your room."

Trying not to show surprise that they would be allowed to stay in the same room together, they followed Carlos to a bedroom at the end of a long hallway.

"This is your room for the night," Carlos announced as he opened the door to a large bedroom.

"This bedroom has its own bathroom," Carlos said, waving his arm in a sweeping gesture, "As you can see, you have everything you need, a king size bed, even fresh towels."

"Thank you... I guess," Sandy said hesitatingly.

Carlos laughed. "Mr. and Mrs. Riley, I am, as you see, the most hospitable kidnapper you will ever meet."

With that, Carlos bid them "good night," and closed the door behind him.

Sandy looked up at Tanner with an expression of confusion. "This is weird."

Seconds later, they heard a knock at their door. Tanner reached down to open the door, but realized that there was no door knob. Carlos opened the door and leaned into the open doorway.

"One more thing," Carlos said without a smile, "I must remind you that your door will be locked, the windows are barred, my men are armed and I have two very unfriendly dogs outside. Please, for your own safety, do not try anything foolish, OK?"

Without waiting for a reply, Carlos shut the door and locked it behind him with a resounding 'click, click.'

"What have we gotten ourselves into?" Sandy asked, in bewilderment.

She and Tanner walked around the room, examining their prison for the night. Looking out the single window of the bedroom, Tanner could see nothing in the blackness of night, but could plainly make out the steel bars on the window.

"What if they kill us?" Sandy said, as the rising level of fear began to show in her eyes.

Tanner pulled his wife to him and embraced her.

"We'll figure out something," he assured her.

"I just want to go home," Sandy cried. "I'm scared."

"I know babe," Tanner reassured her. "We'll be alright, I promise."

"I'm too tired to think about it," Sandy sighed, "I'm going to take a shower and go to bed." She walked over to the bed and pushed down on the mattress, then pulled back the bedspread and covers.

"Probably has bed bugs!"

The next morning Tanner awoke first. He wondered what the time was, but guessed that it must be around 6 a.m. As he laid on the bed, staring at the ceiling, he suddenly bolted upright, flinging the covers back and stood up with a single abrupt motion that woke Sandy from a sound sleep.

"Are you alright?"

"Yeah, I'm… I'm fine," Tanner said, focusing on the ceiling.

"What are you looking at?" Sandy asked.

Tanner was examining the ceiling just above their bed.

"Check this out," he said, pointing up to the ceiling.

"What is it?"

"I think it's an attic access."

He moved in a complete circle, examining the nearly invisible square access door in the ceiling. Like the ceiling, it was covered with a textured 'popcorn' coating.

"I wish I had a flashlight." Tanner whispered.

Sandy, sprung out of the bed and walked across the room to her purse, perched on a dresser. She brought the purse back to the bed and emptied its contents onto the bedspread.

"We can thank Jonathan for this," she said, holding up a black ballpoint pen with 'Taylor & Randall' etched on the side. "I made fun of Jonathan when he bought these pens," she chuckled. Pulling off the cap and pushing a small plastic button at the end of the pen, a small light glowed brightly from its tip.

"Beautiful," Tanner whispered, "Now, I've got to get up there."

Walking across the room, he gently pulled the dresser away from the wall.

"Give me a hand with this," he said, pulling it carefully across ten feet of hardwood floor of the bedroom. Tanner stepped up onto the bed and then crawled on top of the dresser. Carefully standing up, he could examine the square panel closely. He pushed up on the panel and felt if give slightly. Pushing harder, he felt it break away and lift upwards.

"I need to get up a little higher."

"Here, try this chair."

Sandy picked up a chair from across the room and lifted it up to Tanner.

"Not much room for error here," he said as he positioned the chair legs on the top of the narrow dresser.

"Please be careful," Sandy whispered as Tanner, like a tightrope walker, eased himself up onto the chair, while simultaneously pushing up on the attic access door. It broke free from its frame with a slight 'crack,' then carefully Tanner set the panel aside next to the entrance.

"Hand me the flashlight."

Clinching the small flashlight in his teeth, Tanner pushed his upper body through the opening and then pushed up with his arms all the way into the 2 foot by 2 foot opening. Looking around, he was surprised to find that the attic area was just about high enough to stand in. Although the glow of the tiny pen was barely strong enough to see the layout of the dusty room, he ventured quietly into the darkness. He made his way toward what appeared to be a square roof vent built into the end wall of a peaked roof. Below the vent was a metal roof that angled down to the yard below. Tanner focused the light on the vent structure and realized that it was actually a screened-over vent. Pushing on the metal screening, he could feel it give. He pushed harder, it gave a little more. He was satisfied that one could push the screen out of the vent and wiggle through the opening to the metal roof below. He then made his way back to the access door and lowered himself down to the chair and then to the dresser, quietly closing the access door behind him.

"What did you see up there?" Sandy asked excitedly.

"When you get up there and follow this wall, you'll get to a square, screened-in vent, Tanner said, pointing out the directions. "We can push out the metal screening and crawl out onto a metal roof and jump down to the ground."

"Let's go now!" Sandy said, under her breath.

"No, now is not a good time. It's getting light outside and they'll see us for sure!"

Tanner snatched the chair off the dresser and put it back against the wall.

"Here, let's get this dresser back where we got it."

As the couple maneuvered the furniture into place, Sandy noticed the wood floor was covered with little specks of ceiling coating, directly under the access door.

"Jeez, look at this mess."

Quickly, Tanner grabbed his pillow from the bed. Using it as a dust mop, he pushed the specks under the bed in two quick passes. Just as he finished his second pass, there was a knock at the bedroom door and Carlos entered.

"Mr. and Mrs. Riley, I hope you had a comfortable night's rest?"

"Yes… we did," Tanner answered, standing next to the bed with the pillow in his hands. "We were just about ready to make up the bed."

"Very well - breakfast is nearly ready, and then we will continue our business meeting. I'll leave the door open for you."

"Thank you," Sandy said, as Carlos left the room.

Quickly, Tanner got down on his hands and knees, scooping the particles of ceiling material into small piles. Sandy retrieved a trash can from the bathroom and together they removed any trace of the particles. Tanner then flushed the evidence down the toilet and rinsed out the trash can.

"Wow, that was close," Tanner whispered.

"Good thing we didn't make a break for it," Sandy added.

A simple breakfast of scrambled eggs, beans and tortillas had been prepared for the group by Luis and Mario. After breakfast it was obvious that Carlos and Antonio were eager to get back to business. Turning on Tanner's computer, he invited the couple to have a seat at the table along with Mario, and Antonio.

"Mr. Riley, my first question to you this morning is this: Would it be possible for you to teach young Mario here, everything necessary for us to win the California lottery?"

Tanner knew that this was the moment that was critical to his and Sandy's survival. He must never let himself become expendable.

"Let me assure you that I can teach Mario everything about organizing and carrying out the winning of a lottery. However, the

148

mathematics behind these very complicated programs and algorithms requires years of training and experience. You have the tools to do the job, but without my constant refinement and fine tuning of the numbers you will run the risk of losing every lottery you enter. There is no way you can do this on your own, without my level of mathematics, not to mention my computer programming ability."

"So as I see it Mr. Riley," Antonio interjected, "we need to train a team to do the legwork, while you provide the computer skills."

"That would be the only way to do it," Tanner replied.

"Explain to us, then, how you organized your team," Carlos asked.

"Well, we worked with a team of four - myself, Sandy, my brother in law and his wife."

The couple explained the plan, from start to finish. Tanner emphasized the importance of the close teamwork necessary to enlist the cooperation of 25 lottery ticket merchants within a closely defined area. He also explained the incentive of $500 to each manager, to expedite the processing of 10,000 tickets.

By the end of the morning, Carlos, Antonio and Mario withdrew into another room to finalize their decision. After an hour, the men returned to the room to lay out their plan.

"Mr. and Mrs. Riley," Carlos began, "we have decided that we will form a team that will work your lottery plan in San Diego. We want you to train Mario in every aspect of the project, and to work side by side with him. And we want Sandy to do the same with Luis.

Tanner looked across the table at the men and reminded himself that his reply must be firm and without fear.

"Gentlemen, the only thing I am asking, is that Sandy and I be released without harm."

"Mr. Riley," Carlos responded, "you have my word that after we have won this lottery, you and Mrs. Riley will be free to return to your home."

"How can we trust you?" Sandy asked. "How do we know that you won't simply kill us?"

"Mrs. Riley, I understand your concern," Antonio said as he stood up. He walked towards Sandy, waving his cigar as he spoke.

"You are to us like the goose that laid the golden eggs. You are familiar with that famous fable I assume?" The gray haired man continued without waiting for an answer.

"We would be stupid to kill you and your husband. You are much more valuable to us alive. Please understand – we don't wish to harm you or your husband. We only want your cooperation for a short period of time."

"And then, after helping you, you promise that we can go home?" Sandy's reply was both a statement and a question.

"That is our promise," Antonio answered.

"Yes," Mario added.

"Absolutely," Carlos said.

Carlos and his men immediately launched their plan into action. That very day they returned through the Tecate tunnel and drove to San Diego, where Carlos had arranged for the group to set up their headquarters at an isolated beach house.

Carlos and Antonio had been monitoring the quickly growing SuperLotto jackpot for a few weeks, which by now, Thursday, had grown to $50 million. If no winner claimed the jackpot this Saturday they determined to try for the estimated win of $52 million on the following Wednesday. That would give the team four days to purchase 250,000 tickets. It was the exact scenario of Tanner and Sandy's big win in Huntington Beach a few months earlier.

Both pairs were provided rental cars and operating cash. Tanner and Luis were given $3000 cash to set up two computers and two printers for the processing of the play slips.

Tanner was surprised with how smoothly Mario and Luis adapted to the tasks of locating and setting up Lottery retailers and gathering thousands of play slips. The teams worked 12 hours on both Friday and Saturday.

On Saturday evening the team was joined by Carlos and Antonio in a nearby hotel bar to see the results of the SuperLotto game. Most of the men were intoxicated by the time the draw was announced. Tanner monitored the game results on his laptop and at 8 p.m. he announced to the men that there was no winner. The men began celebrating loudly in the crowded bar, patting each other on the back and high-fiving between buying round after round of drinks. It was late when the group finally turned in for the night, but the team of 4 knew that the hardest part was about to start Sunday morning.

Sunday, Monday, Tuesday and Wednesday flew by in a flurry of activity. After Tanner finalized his calculations and his program finally generated a fresh list of 250,000 numbers, it was a race against Wednesday to print 50,000 play slips, distribute them to the lottery retailers and pay for them in cash. Because of Tanner's and Sandy's experience, the whole process went smoothly. Mario and Luis proved to be both fast learners and hard workers.

On Wednesday evening the entire group met at the beach house with a mountain of lottery tickets stacked on top of a queen-sized bed.

Antonio brought a case of champagne and a box of Cuban cigars. Carlos, ready to celebrate, carried a bottle of Tres Generaciones Tequila.

Tanner and Sandy, however, were in no such celebratory frame of mind. Although Tanner had done his very best in generating this new list of numbers, he feared the possible consequences of failure.

Would Carlos and Antonio give them another chance? Sandy, too, was fearful of their captor's reaction to failure. They had worked so hard for these men, with the precious goal of freedom their only reward.

As Tanner turned on his computer he recalled the excitement that he and Sandy had experienced along with Jonathan and Carolyn a few months before. How different this was, in a room of ruthless armed kidnappers, expecting to become instant millionaires. At 8 p.m. the four men grouped around Tanner as he opened up the California lottery website.

"This might take a few minutes," Sandy assured the men. "The results usually appear between now and 8:15."

"Let's hope we'll be opening the champagne by 8:16," Carlos said with a smile.

Refreshing the screen every minute or so, Tanner monitored the results page until 8:08 when the results started to filter in.

"Here we go," Tanner shouted. The men moved closer behind Tanner and Sandy.

"There appears to be one winner."

"The winning ticket was purchased at Miller's Downtown Liquor."

"That's one of our stores," Luis shouted to Sandy excitedly.

"Here come the numbers… write these down Sandy!"

Sandy grabbed a pen from her purse and began scribbling down the numbers on the palm of her hand.

"12 – 13 – 27 - 31 – 44 – and the bonus number is 17, got it?"

"Got it," Sandy shouted.

Tanner opened up his data page and started typing in the numbers as Sandy repeated them. After carefully typing in the numbers into the search box and hitting ENTER, the screen almost instantly found a match.

"Bingo! - We've got a match!" Tanner shouted.

The men looked at each other. At first, there was a second of confusion.

"Bingo?" Antonio repeated.

"We won old man!" Carlos shouted. *"We did it - there is a match!"*

The scene inside the beach house turned into bedlam – resembling a World Series locker room celebration. The men, beside themselves with exuberance, began uncorking the champagne and passing the open bottles to everyone in the room. Tanner, congratulated profusely by each of the men, was hugged, high-fived and slapped him on the back. Each uttered their various versions of congratulations in Spanish.

Antonio passed the Cuban cigars to each person, including Sandy. Carlos broke out the Tequila and poured several shots for the men. After several minutes of celebration, Tanner announced that it was time to search for the winning lottery ticket. He directed the men to the piles of ticket bundles stacked on the bed. Finding the pile of tickets marked 'Miller's Downtown Liquor,' he did his best to direct the attention of the half-drunk men.

"Ok, everyone grab a bundle of tickets and start looking for this number," he shouted. Sandy wrote out the winning numbers on a torn scrap of a grocery bag.

"12 – 13 – 27 - 31 – 44 – and 17. Just check each ticket for the last number of 17," she shouted to the men.

"Look for 17?" Antonio asked.

"On the ticket, look at the last number to be 17," Mario explained to Tony. "It's faster that way."

After the group spent 20 minutes shuffling through thousands of tickets, Carlos finally held a lottery ticket over his head and began shouting, *"Here it is muchachos!* Here's the 52 million dollar ticket!"

Putting on his reading glasses, Carlos examined it closely, while Antonio read off the numbers from Sandy's scrap of paper.

"12"

"Yes"

"13"

"Si, 13"

"27"

"27, yes,"

"31"

"31, si,"

"Number 44,"

"Yes, 44,"

"And the bonus number, 17."

After confirming the numbers, the room again exploded into delirious excitement. Mario religiously crossed his chest, while gazing skyward, and while Antonio, with his cigar in hand, raised his hands upwards in what appeared to be heavenly thankfulness. Next, the ticket was handed to Antonio for examination.

"Can you imagine, this little piece of paper is worth $52 million?" Antonio exclaimed.

Mario took the ticket and scrutinized every inch of it.

"It's almost like a dream, holding a fortune between my fingers," Mario said, holding the ticket in the air between his thumb and forefinger.

Lastly, Luis was handed the lottery ticket for his scrutiny. Examining the ticket briefly he casually placed it into his shirt pocket. What happened within the span of the next 15 seconds, no one except Luis was ready for. Pulling his 9 millimeter semi-automatic pistol from his shoulder holster, Luis quickly snapped off two shots nearly point blank into Tony Telemontes' chest. Three more fatal shots sent Carlos rocketing backwards against a wall. Mario, in stunned response, leaped behind a stuffed chair, and in one movement racked a round into the chamber of his pistol and came up firing. Tanner pushed Sandy roughly onto the floor and covered her with his body. Mario and Luis each fired two rounds nearly simultaneously, and both fell to the floor, fatally wounded.

"Please don't kill us!" Sandy screamed. The room had now become eerily silent.

"Baby, are you alright?" Tanner's eyes were filled with panic as he looked at his wife, fearing the worse.

"Yeah... I think so," Sandy responded, sobbing.

Tanner inched his head above the couch to see that no one in the room was moving. Standing up, he surveyed the room. Seconds before, it been the scene of celebration, - now, it reeked from the smell of gunpowder. Carlos, eyes fixed in a stare of death, lay crookedly against a wall just a few feet away. Antonio was lying flat on his back next to Carlos, with two closely spaced chest wounds which, Tanner was certain were also fatal. Across the room, Mario and Luis were laying on their backs. As Tanner carefully approached them, he could see that each had sustained two fatal gunshots.

"Are they dead?" Sandy asked.

Tanner turned to see Sandy, standing across the room, her hands to her face.

"I think all of them are dead," Tanner answered.

"Are you OK?" Sandy said, walking toward her husband.

"Yeah, I'm fine."

"What should we do?" Sandy asked, her voice shaking as she looked around the room.

"I say we get the hell out of here."

Sandy bent down and checked for a pulse on the side of Luis' neck.

"I can't believe it, they are all dead," Sandy said.

"If it weren't for Mario, we would be dead too. Luis would have killed everyone in this room for this ticket," Tanner said as he leaned down and plucked the lottery ticket from Luis' shirt pocket.

"Shouldn't we call the police?" Sandy asked.

"Hell no."

"So, we should just leave then?"

"We should load all of the tickets and all of our belongings in the car and get out of here."

Tanner put the ticket in his pocket. His mind was reeling as he quickly put together their exit strategy.

"The police will figure out who these men are, and will probably assume that this was just another gang rivalry shooting."

"I hope you're right," Sandy said.

He moved to the window and pulled back the curtain. There was no activity outside.

"We need to gather up every single ticket and throw them in the trunk of the car," Tanner said. Finding a large waste basket from the kitchen, Tanner began stuffing it full with bundles of tickets. Sandy quickly assisted and within a few moments the trunk of the rental car was nearly full.

The couple next made certain that all of their belongings were removed from the scene and loaded into the car. Both printers, all of the computers and related equipment, clothing, personal items, and everything else that might tie them to the scene of the shooting were removed. After double checking the beach house, they drove off in the rental car and headed back home.

Before Tanner had driven a mile, he exited the freeway and pulled into a parking lot.

"Why are you stopping?" Sandy asked.

Tanner parked the car and turned off the ignition.

"We can't take this car," he said. "It was rented by Carlos. - We've got to rent another car and take this one back to the beach house. And we've got to do it quickly, before someone discovers what happened."

The couple drove for nearly a half hour before finding a car rental agency. Within an hour they had transferred their belongings to the new rental and returned Carlos' car to the beach house. After wiping down the car for fingerprints, Tanner and Sandy finally resumed their escape back to Huntington Beach.

Chapter 17

The Tanner and Sandra Riley Foundation

When the San Diego police were finally called to the scene of the beach house killings, the four dead men were quickly identified as Tijuana cartel members. It was assumed by the investigators that the shootout was not unlike dozens of other similar gang related deaths in the drug cartel world.

For the Arellano Felix organization, the death of Carlos "Fat Man" Flores and Tony Telemontes was a major loss as well as a mystery. Carlos and Antonio had kept this operation quiet, with the intention of surprising their bosses only after successfully winning the lottery jackpot. Only four men in the Tijuana cartel were aware of the existence of Tanner Riley's amazing computer programs, and all four were dead.

The kidnapping and subsequent lottery win in San Diego were never spoken of by the couple, not even to Jonathan and Carolyn. Upon returning home, Tanner and Sandy tried to put their frightful experience behind them and resume their normal routine, except for one last important detail.

It would have been impossible for Tanner or Sandy to claim the $52 million jackpot. The notoriety would be enormous, triggering investigations that would surely alter the future of lottery organizations around the world. Together, they decided on a plan for the tainted lottery ticket that could transform the terrible experience into something beneficial to thousands of families.

Over the years, working at Children's Hospital, Sandy had developed close relationships with many important people in the medical community. However, this plan would require the discreet assistance of a very trustworthy individual. Doctor Sam, one of

Sandy's long-time mentors and trusted friends, naturally came to mind.

Doctor Sam, although retired from medicine, had recently established a charitable foundation for Children's Hospital of Orange County, where he had practiced for many years. It was Doctor Sam who volunteered his own surgical talents and helped Sandy over the years recruit other doctors and skilled nurses to assist with extreme hardship cases. Sandy was also aware that Dr. Sam, having been born in Mexico, was passionately involved with a new, children's hospital in Baja California named Hospital *Infantil de Californias.* Located in Tijuana, the new facility boasted three surgical rooms, modern equipment and the growing capability to treat needy children from all over Baja California, and Mexico. Doctor Sam's charitable foundation called, *'Puente de los niños'*, or *'Children's Bridge'*, raised funds for both hospitals.

Sandy instinctively knew Dr. Sam would be the man that she could trust with the couple's plan. But how, they wondered, could they explain the winning ticket to him – and their wish to contribute the entire amount to the two children's hospitals? They decided to invite Dr. Sam to their home for dinner.

Dr. Sam, a widower in his eighties, was delighted to accept the invitation to dinner at the Riley's home. He had not seen Sandy since learning of the couple's lottery win, and was eager to learn all about it. On his drive to dinner, the possibility that the new lottery millionaires were interested in donating to 'Puente de los niños' crossed his mind.

Upon ringing the doorbell, the doctor was greeted by Sandy, smiling broadly.

"Hello Doctor," she said as she hugged the tall, but slightly built man. "It's so good to see you."

"And I am delighted to see you too Sandy. Thank you for inviting me."

The doctor handed Sandy a bottle of wine as he entered the hallway.

"This is my favorite wine," the doctor said, "it's said to be one of the top 10 Merlots produced in California."

"Thank you," Sandy said. "This will go perfect with the rib-eye steaks that Tanner is barbequing back here."

Sandy led the doctor through the living room onto the patio, where Tanner was standing at the barbeque, tending to the steaks.

"Tanner, good to see you young man!" the doctor said, walking across the patio, holding out his hand to shake Tanner's.

"Nice to see you too, Doctor Sam," Tanner said, shaking his hand. "It's been a few months, hasn't it?"

"Yes, it has. I've not seen you two since you've made your millions in the lottery. I can't even imagine what that would be like," the doctor said. "Although, looking at you two, I must say that wealth becomes you."

"Well, strangely enough, that is what we wanted to talk to you about," Sandy said.

"Now you've got me curious," the doctor replied.

"Let's go inside and open this wine while Tanner finishes up with these steaks," Sandy suggested.

"Honey, I'm ready with the potatoes, the salad and the garlic toast, OK?" Sandy announced, as she and the doctor walked back into the house.

Tanner deftly plucked the sizzling steaks off of the grill and placed them on a platter.

"These are perfect and ready to go," he shouted, turning off the grill and gathering up the utensils. "Pour the wine, it's time to eat!"

That evening the doctor recounted some of the fond memories of his years at CHOC. He met Sandy a few years before his retirement and it was evident that the two shared great respect for one another. Sandy, however, was most interested in the doctor's current work with the children's hospital in Tijuana.

"Sandy, you and Tanner really must come down to visit the hospital. I would love to give you a tour and show you the progress that is going on down there," the doctor said. "You would be very impressed."

"We would love to visit," Tanner said. "Sandy and I have heard amazing things about it for over a year now."

"That is one of the reasons that we wanted to get together with you this evening," Sandy interjected. "We've both decided to make a significant contribution to the foundation."

The doctor smiled.

"I had a feeling, as soon as I received your invitation, that you two might be interested in making a donation. That makes me very happy, Sandy."

"And, Doctor Sam, you are correct," Sandy said, reaching out and touching the elderly man's hand. "But the contribution we want to make is a little complicated," she said.

"Sandy," the doctor responded. "Anything at all that you wish to give will be very much appreciated."

"What Sandy means by our donation being a little complicated is that we wish to remain completely anonymous. We want you to be the donor," Tanner said.

The doctor's facial expression turned inquisitive.

"I'm not sure what you mean," he said.

Tanner slid a folder across the table towards the doctor.

"This might help."

"What's this?" the doctor asked. He reached into his shirt pocket for his reading glasses.

"Go ahead, open it," Tanner replied.

Opening the manila folder the doctor saw a newspaper clipping with a lottery ticket paper-clipped to it.

"Read the words that are highlighted on the clipping," Tanner said, – a smile crossing his face as he watched the doctor examine the contents of the folder.

The doctor picked up the clipping and started reading the part highlighted in yellow.

"Lottery results for Wednesday. There was one winning ticket for Wednesday's SuperLotto Plus game. The winning ticket, valued at $52 million, was purchased at Miller's Liquor in downtown San Diego. The winning numbers were: 12 – 13 – 27 - 31 – 44 –17." The winner has yet to be identified."

The elderly doctor's hand began to tremble slightly as he picked up the lottery ticket and read the corresponding numbers: 12-13-27-31-44-17.

"My God Tanner, this is a winning ticket."

"Doctor, *this is now your winning ticket.* We want to give it to you - to claim as the legal owner. You can then determine the best way to allocate the funds through your foundation."

"The money is yours," Sandy repeated reassuringly.

The doctor stumbled for words.

"But I don't understand, how did you..."

Tanner leaned forward to interrupt the doctor.

"All we can tell you is, someone walked into Miller's Downtown Liquor in San Diego three months ago and bought this ticket. Unfortunately, this person has recently passed away, and with no uncertainty, the purchaser of this ticket requested you to claim it and the winnings to go to *Puente de los niños.*"

The explanation given by the couple, although not entirely accurate, was truthful for the most part. In actuality, Sandy, along with the murderous Luis Figeroa, were indeed the ones who walked into Miller's Downtown Liquor and purchased the winning lottery ticket. Luis Figeroa did, in fact, recently pass away, and Sandy, the co-purchaser of the ticket, did request that the proceeds go to Doctor Sam and *'Puente de los niños.'*

One week later, Doctor Sam walked into the Santa Ana Office of the California Lottery to make his claim.

"Good morning sir, how can I help you this morning?" the receptionist said with a perky tone to her voice.

"Good morning," the doctor said. "I'm here to claim my winning ticket for the SuperLotto Plus drawing." Doctor Sam removed the lottery ticket from the envelope. The ticket trembled slightly in his hand as he placed it on the counter. The receptionist smiling broadly walked from her desk to the counter and picked up the ticket.

"Oh, my!" she said, flipping over the ticket and examining both sides. "We've been wondering when this ticket would be claimed! May I be the first to congratulate you?" She reached across the counter to shake hands with the doctor.

"I'm Rita Ellis," she said, in an animated voice, as she shook the doctor's hand. She seemed genuinely excited and happy to meet him.

The claiming procedure continued ever so smoothly, and within a few weeks Doctor Sam received his windfall in the form of a check. The net amount of $21,294,300, represented the single cash payout option, minus federal taxes.

The good doctor was applauded nationwide for his generous decision to donate every dime of his lottery winnings to his own foundation.

Hospital Infantil de Californias received a record breaking donation of $11 million, allowing for much needed expansion, including the hiring and training of more staff.

Children's Hospital of Orange County received the balance of the winning lottery jackpot – some $10 million.

Whenever Sandy enters the Children's Hospital of Orange County, she cannot help but feel pleased as she passes through the hallway where a beautiful bronze plaque hangs, commemorating the outstanding philanthropy of Doctor Sam.

***

There is no question that winning the lottery was a life-changing event for the Rileys. Most of the changes experienced by the couple were positive. But who could have predicted the unbridled greed of a few men, leading to Tanner and Sandy's abduction? And who indeed could have guessed that one of these greedy kidnappers would be willing to murder, in cold blood, three of his peers for the winning ticket?

Having lived through these incredibly difficult events, Tanner and Sandy have remained, remarkably normal. They have watched the best and most exciting chapter in their lives go very bad, within months of their lottery win. And, in a 180 degree shift, they witnessed their most horrific experience, transformed into something benevolent.

There is comfort too, in that there are four less criminal cartel members in the world. To what extent the criminal activities of these men have been affected, we may never fully know.

Both Sandy and Tanner agreed that, in a strange way, the results of the second lottery win were the most satisfying. The first lottery win transformed the couple's lifestyle into millionaire status. The results of the second win, however, resulted in the satisfaction of giving tens of millions of dollars to the charities that were closest to Sandy's heart.

Over the months, watching the expansion of *Hospital Infantil de Californias* was so exciting for the couple, Sandy began suggesting the possibility of starting their own charitable foundation.

On the drive home from one of their trips to Tijuana, Sandy expressed her wish to do more.

"Do you remember when I asked you what we would do with the money if we won the lottery?"

"I do," Tanner said. "I told you that you could do anything that you wanted to do. And I remember you said that you wanted to help people that were less fortunate than you."

Sandy leaned in closer and kissed Tanner on the cheek.

"I had no idea when I asked you that question that I would be doing this."

"Does it make you happy?"

"I'm very happy," Sandy said. "And I love you for making it possible. I'm so proud of you."

"It almost got us killed." Tanner said regretfully.

"But we didn't, and that's what matters."

"So what do you think our next step should be?" Tanner asked.

"I'm only sure of one thing," Sandy replied. "I want to be more involved with projects like Hospital Infantil. I've never experienced more…happiness - more personal satisfaction with any other work."

Tanner could hear that wonderful conviction in his wife's voice. Sandy, the altruistic research nurse, had found the sweet spot of her career. Now it was Tanner's turn.

"I've been talking to Richard Stewart about the process of setting up a private foundation." Tanner said. "He says that we should have no problem, and he will have a plan for us to examine within a couple of weeks."

"What shall we call it?" Sandy asked with delight.

"The Tanner and Sandra Riley Foundation, of course," Tanner said.

"That has a nice sound – *The Tanner and Sandra Riley foundation.* I like that!" Sandra exclaimed.

"But more important than the name of our new foundation, is how we will fund it. I've kinda' been working on that too. Would you like to hear my Tanner and Sandra Riley Foundation' business plan for the next year and a half?"

"Go ahead, Mr. Riley, I'm ready to be impressed," Sandy announced.

"The first step would be hiring four good people, maybe college students, smart kids with good backgrounds. Straight A students with big dreams."

"Premed students!" Sandy shouted, interrupting Tanners momentum.

"Yes, top notch kids that we vet thoroughly – background checks, drug tests, polygraph, you name it. We guarantee them each $250,000 for the summer, enough to pay off all their student loans.

We play four lotteries, here in California, with the same team. Each one of the teams takes turns claiming the winning ticket. We have them sign an iron-clad non-disclosure agreement and a contract that they agree to donate all their winnings to our foundation – minus their cut of $500,000. At the end of their contract, each of the four team members will have earned $750,000."

Tanner finished, took a breath and glanced over at Sandy.

"What do you think?"

Sandy pursed her lips together and nodded her head in approval.

"What if one of them does a 'Luis Figeroa' on us – or demands half, or all the jackpot? What do we do if one of them threatens to go to the Lottery commission, to kill the goose that lays the golden eggs?"

Sandy's role as Devil's advocate was no surprise to Tanner. She had a knack for poking holes in the best laid plans.

"Those are all great questions my dear - and I've given each of these scenarios quite a bit of thought," Tanner countered.

"Why does that not surprise me?" Sandy said.

"First of all, a repeat of what Luis Figeroa did in San Diego, may be normal in the drug cartel world, but certainly not among straight 'A,' clean-cut college kids. Their loyalty to us will be well-rewarded with more money than most of them will make in their first 10 years out of college. But to insure their loyalty and confidentiality, we will offer the same team members $2 million each for the following summer, when we move our lottery program to Europe - all expenses included, of course."

"We're taking our whole team to Europe?"

"Yup," Tanner said, "I've been charting the EuroLottery for a few weeks and I'm convinced that it may have slightly better odds than that of California lotteries."

"And after Europe, what?"

"After Europe, I'm done," Tanner said, with a wry grin.

"Done?"

"Well, unless we recruit another team and start over with 4 more lottery winners."

By summer break, the Riley's did indeed manage to put together a team of four students from 4 Southern California colleges. Working from June through August, the team purchased one million lottery tickets divided among four games. Each member, as agreed, claimed a winning lottery ticket. After settling with each of the team members, The Tanner and Sandy Riley Foundation netted nearly $30 million after taxes.

Less than a year later, the same team moved their operations to London, England, where they proceeded to repeat their success with the EuroLottery. Each of the team members returned home with $2 million. At the same time, the Riley's foundation expanded financially by another $52 million.

With a war chest of nearly $100 million, Tanner and Sandy took a break from the lottery for a while. The Tanner and Sandy Riley Foundation continues to help thousands of children and their parents throughout the United States and Mexico. The foundation has also donated over 3 million frequent flyer miles to families in need of emergency medical travel. Having built three clinics in Southern California, with two more in the planning stages, Sandy is enjoying a very busy life, doing what she loves the most.

Tanner has retired from his job and now, alongside Sandy, devotes most of his time and energies to the foundation.

Both Tanner and Sandy have mastered the art, and joy of giving on a personal basis, too.

On a trip to Disneyland, with Jonathan and Carolyn, they stood in line for tickets in front of a family of five. While eavesdropping on their conversation, Sandy discerned that the family was on a very limited budget. Sandy engaged the mother in conversation and soon decided what she wanted to do. After paying for themselves, Sandy told the ticket clerk,

"Please include the family of five, behind us, on our credit card. Make it a 2 day hopper pass for all of them, please."

By the time the family discovered that their 2-day Disneyland vacation had been paid in full, Sandy, Tanner, Jonathan and Carolyn had disappeared into the crowd through the main entrance gate.

"That was almost intoxicating!" Sandy exclaimed.

"Imagine how relieved they are right now," Tanner said. "Now they can really enjoy their vacation!"

The generous gift to that family of five gave them so much satisfaction, the couple now routinely looks for opportunities to help other hard-working families, who could use a helping hand.

One of Tanner's most satisfying acts of generosity happened the day he heard that a workmate of his had died of an unexpected heart attack. The devastated wife and 3 children, he learned, were left with no life insurance and a house that had been heavily mortgaged. That very day, Tanner called his Goldman agent and arranged for the family's $230,000 mortgage to be paid in full.

Not to be outdone, Sandy, once observed at the local gas station, a young woman, standing beside her broken-down car with the hood up. Two children were sitting in the back seat, and Sandy could see that the poor woman was crying. Sandy helped the young woman by calling a tow truck for her, and arranged for the car to be taken to the local Toyota dealer. She drove to meet them and determined that the old car which the young mother was driving, wasn't worth repairing. Stalling for time, Sandy had the family wait in the dealer's waiting room, telling the woman that the car was being checked out for needed repairs. Within an hour, Sandy picked out a new Toyota Sienna van for the family and wrote a check for $35,000 to the dealership. Sandy finished her business with the salesman and disappeared by the time the salesman announced to the young mother that the family was now the proud owner of a brand new van.

Tanner and Sandy have both learned the truth in what one writer once expressed - "The thrill of taking lasts a day. The thrill of giving lasts a lifetime."

There is no question that winning the lottery is one of the most thrilling events one can have in their lifetime. Tanner, in fact, is planning for one more of these thrilling events. Powerball.

Writing a program to attack this juggernaut of a game will take some time, but the billion-dollar plus payout will be worth the effort. It will require, as Tanner estimates it, another year of research, programming and testing and a $2 million ante.

Look for the name of Sandy Riley to appear in the news someday soon. She will be the official claimant. The news story will be interesting indeed. The 11 o'clock news teaser will announce:

"What are the chances that the wife of a former $86 million Superlotto winner would win the billion dollar plus Powerball lottery? The story at 11."

But then, you already know the story.

www.ingramcontent.com/pod-product-compliance
Lightning Source LLC
Chambersburg PA
CBHW070324130626
46556CB00007B/2723